WAR MAIDEN

THE FIRE HEART CHRONICLES BOOK 6

JULIANA HAYGERT

COPYRIGHT

This book is a work of fiction. Names, characters, places, and incidents either are products of the author's imagination or are used fictitiously. Any resemblance to actual persons, living or dead, events, or locales is entirely coincidental.

Manufactured in the United States of America.

First Edition May 2019

www.JulianaHaygert.com

Edited by H. Danielle Crabtree

Cover design by Ravven

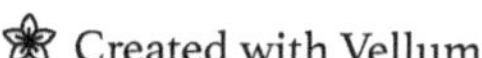 Created with Vellum

AUTHOR'S NOTE

DICTIONARY

Chey – daughter
Chini – son
Daj – mother
Dat – father
Gadjo – non-Romani person
Nais tuke – thank you
Ozi – fire
Phal – brother
Phen – sister
Puri Chey – granddaughter
Puri Chini – grandson
Puri Daj – grandmother
Puri Dat – grandfather
Rom Baro – leader of the enclave
Ruv – wolf/werewolf
Saint Sara-la-Kali – Romani Saint
Sastimos – a greeting
Vurdon – wagon

Yog – fire
Yog Ozi Nas – fire heart fever

1

As normal as they could be after all that had happened the past few weeks.

Letting out a long sigh, I glanced up at the three-story house in front of me. I racked my mind, trying to think of something else I could be doing instead of going inside—there was plenty to be done—but I couldn't delay it anymore.

I climbed up the three steps to the front door, and Rick and Joel stepped aside.

"Any changes?"

"No," Joel said. "They have been quiet in there."

"Good," I muttered, reaching for the knob.

The door opened with a click, and dreading the next few minutes, I pushed inside.

"There you are!" Darcy exclaimed, rushing toward me with wide eyes. Her long white hair was loose and knotty, her clothes seemed rumpled, and her cheeks were hollow. Hadn't she been eating? Or sleeping? "I've been calling for you for days now." She grabbed my arm with both her hands.

"I know." I pulled my arm from her grip and took a step back. "What the hell do you want?"

Darcy frowned. "Is that the way to talk to your elders, heart maiden?"

"To the crazy one who tried to kill her own granddaughter, yes, it is."

Darcy flinched.

Two weeks ago, Darcy had lost it, along with the rest of the elder council members. They had attacked me, accusing me of being mad—which wasn't entirely false. But when I refused to let them take me, to kill me, she retaliated. Darcy attacked her own people, the tziganes she had seen grow up in the Lovell enclave, and even Ryane, her granddaughter. My instinct had been to kill her and the others, but unlike them, I liked to think I was a considerate and mostly a sane person. I didn't kill so easily.

So, after a couple of nights in jail—because they deserved to feel like criminals—I had moved the elder council members to this house at the edge of the enclave. It had been empty for a while, and since it was a big place with many rooms, it would serve as a comfortable prison. My grandmother, Sheila, my mother, Marisa, my father, Dolan, and a few other powerful tziganes had helped me with its magical protection. The windows and doors didn't open for the people locked inside, no matter what they tried—magic or brute force. Only a handful of people had the power to open the doors and windows, but only one of them came daily to check on them and bring food.

Ryane. Despite having her *puri daj* take her by the throat, the young woman hadn't given up on her family. She hoped her grandmother and her father, Oscar, would apologize and become the elders they were meant to be.

I didn't say anything because I didn't want to see Ryane sad, but even her brother, Artan, knew Darcy and Oscar wouldn't repent. Not that easily.

Moreover, I wouldn't forgive them. Or trust them. As the temporary leader of the enclave, I had to think of the safety of the majority, and the former elder council members were a threat to all of us.

Darcy reached for me again and I noticed her hands shaking. "Mirella," she started. I took another step back, keeping out of her reach. She lowered her hands. "Listen to me. You have to let us out."

I snorted. "Really? You called me here to ask me to release you? After what you did?"

"You don't understand. We have to get out of here. Everyone."

I frowned. "What do you mean?"

She pressed a hand to her chest. "I can feel it. Something big is coming. Damara is planning something awful and all of us need to run."

"What are you now? Some kind of oracle?"

Darcy clutched her hands in a plea. "I beg you. Let us go. We'll leave and never look back."

Did she really think I would buy this act? "Stop, Darcy. I don't have time for your nonsense."

I turned to the door, but she grabbed my hands again. "Mirella, you—"

"Let me go." I jerked my hand free, ready to call my fire if I had to defend myself.

But instead of attacking me, Darcy fell to her knees. "Please, Mirella."

I stared at the old hag, confused. This was so unlike her.

In the nine months I had been the heart maiden, I had never seen her like this.

"Mother." Oscar appeared from the living room and rushed to the old hag. He grabbed her shoulders and helped her up. "She has been babbling nonsense for the last few days."

Darcy leaned on her son's shoulders. "Tell her, Oscar. Tell her what I've been feeling."

Oscar shook his head. "I honestly don't know what she's talking about. I'm sorry, Mirella." He carried her back, whispering soothing words to her.

The hair on my arms stood on end as a chill rolled down my spine. I glanced around and found the other elder council members watching me—from the archway leading to the dining room, from the kitchen in the back, and from the second floor's landing.

What? Had they gone mad too, or were they shocked by Darcy's behavior?

Feeling uncomfortable, I dashed from the house.

"Everything okay?" Rick asked, eyes narrowed.

I took in a long, calming breath, and nodded. "Yes, everything is okay."

Before he could say anything else, I walked away. Away from that cursed house and Darcy and her craziness.

Who was I to talk? If it weren't for Kane, I would be the one being assaulted by visions and acting like a mad woman.

Kane ...

My heart sank.

Two weeks ago, Artan's wife died from ingesting poison intended for me. Instantly, Artan fell into despair. I went to see him, to help him, to try and sooth him, but instead, he kissed me.

And I ended up kissing him back.

It had been for only a few seconds, but I had allowed him to kiss me. I felt guilt over his loss. But in the end, I pushed him away.

But Artan boasted about the kiss to Kane, saying I had been the one to kiss him first.

I tried to explain things to Kane, but I hadn't known how. Trina, the one who left the poison for me, had broken Kane's heart. They had been married and she cheated on him.

And I had kissed Artan, bringing that terrible feeling of betrayal he had so desperately tried to bury back to the surface.

I knew Kane was still in Lovell, since my madness, a side effect of the fire heart fever, was contained, but I had barely seen him. And every time we happened to cross paths, he marched away as fast as he could.

Despite my intention to make everything right—to help the new council, to defeat Damara, to avenge our friends, and to gain Kane's trust back—fate wasn't kind to me.

On my way from the prison-house to the main square, I spotted Kane crossing a perpendicular street.

I skidded to a stop as my heart tightened.

As usual, Kane wore all black with his twin swords strapped in an X on his back. His dark brown hair was longer now, and he had a short stubble over his chin and jaw—which only added to his fierce and manly image.

He was handsome, and it hurt to see him and not be able to touch him.

Fate decided to have a laugh and made Kane turn his head in my direction. His piercing hazel eyes met mine. A deep knot appeared between his brows before he sped up his steps and disappeared from my sight.

No matter how much he ran from me, there was no escape now. He was going to the same place I was.

But that didn't mean I had to rush there too.

Slowing my steps, I glanced up at the beautiful darkening blue sky and inhaled deeply. Spring was in full effect, and the scent of wildflowers and pine trees filled my nostrils, calming me.

I was walking by the fountain in the main square when Lash, one of the warriors, approached me.

"This arrived a few minutes ago," he said, handing me a folded paper.

"Thanks," I said, taking it from him.

I already knew what it was. A note from Ramon. He sent those every couple of days, wanting to check on us and let us know he and his pack were okay. Because of me, their den had been destroyed by Damara, and they had to flee. Right now, they were camped at the foot of a mountain, but Ramon assured me they would soon clear out the den and move back.

I let out a sigh. So many people had been affected because of my fight with Damara. If only I could challenge her to a duel and be done with everything. But she would never agree to that. The older heart maiden was proud, and the madness had already taken her mind many, many years ago. She would stop at nothing now. She would destroy not only me, but everyone who stood with me.

Unless I stopped her first.

Despite my best effort, my heart raced anew once I entered the main building in the square, and approached the council room. I paused at the half-open door and took another long breath.

Then I walked inside.

My family and friends were seated in the council chairs—Marisa, Dolan, Sheila, Theron, Ellie, Artan, Rye, Cora, and Kane.

My mother and my father occupied the center chairs, with Sheila right beside them. I narrowed my eyes, observing how my father turned to my mother, how he looked at her, as if she was the only woman in the world. They had been a little too close the past couple of weeks, and I wasn't sure how to feel about it.

Theron and Ellie didn't disguise they were dating. They sat side-by-side, hands entwined, and often smiled at each other.

Unlike Cora and Rye, who despite being practically together for almost four years, still hadn't assumed their relationship. Cora sat beside Rye, but her body language was hard and cold, and she kept her back slightly turned to the warrior. Poor Rye.

Artan was sprawled in his chair, as far away as he could manage from Kane, his leg over the armrest, his head lolled back. His shirt was buttoned wrong, and his sash was falling around his hips. I didn't have to get close to know he was drunk. Again.

Kane was the only one standing. I didn't know if it was because he had just arrived too, or because he was tense knowing I would be here, but he seemed too worked up.

"Here she comes," my mother said, spotting me. "I'm sure she can help us decide."

I approached the chairs. "Help with what?"

"The enclave is mostly under order right now," Dolan started. "And we need to decide our next move."

"How and when are we going after Damara?" Sheila asked.

"We don't even know where she is," Theron said. As the leader of the warriors, he had been conducting stealth scouting through the forest, trying to locate Damara and her minions. "Until we actually find her, we can't attack her."

"We're sitting ducks," Cora said.

"Unfortunately, there isn't much we can do about that," Rye said. Cora shot him a glare, but he shrugged. "It's true. All we can do is make sure our perimeter is strong so they can't attack us here."

"We've been checking the magic around the perimeter twice a day," Sheila said. As her magic was incredible, she was the one overseeing that. "It's as strong as can be."

"Then we have nothing to worry about," I said. Why didn't I feel like it, though? If I could, I would hide them all. Take them far away. Disappear from this continent so Damara couldn't find them.

Then I would come back for her.

The half-open door banged on the wall as Leander ran inside the room, out of breath. "Mirella, council," he wheezed.

I frowned at him, afraid of what he would say. "What is it?"

"They are here," he rasped. "The alchemists are here."

2

I HESITATED FOR A SECOND.

They were here? The alchemists were here? To attack us? That didn't make sense.

"Are they attacking?" I asked. "What about the border magic?"

Leander shook his head. "They aren't attacking. They are gathered right beside the western border."

Theron shot to his feet. "We should go. Be ready in case they try to attack."

"The magic should hold up," Sheila said, reminding us she had mentioned that a few moments ago. "They can't get in."

"Still, it's suspicious that they are here," Kane said. "We should check it out."

"Agreed," Cora said. She rose to her feet with Rye, their hands going to the hilt of the swords hanging at their hips. Ready for battle. Always.

Meanwhile, I was wearing ripped jeans, a wide shoulder blouse, and flat sandals. I wondered if I could spare a couple of minutes to change into the warrior's uniform. I shook my head, discarding that idea. If it came down to fighting, I would do it regardless of how I was dressed.

"Leander, gather our best warriors and meet us there," Theron said. The young warrior nodded, then rushed out of the room to follow through with the order. Then, Theron turned to us. "Let's go."

Theron took the lead, with Kane beside him. Artan stumbled out of his chair, visibly trying to sober up, but failing. My chest squeezed with the scene. I thought about reaching for him and helping him, but decided it was best if I didn't do anything. Last time I tried to help him, it ended with Kane breaking up with me.

Well, Kane hadn't said it like that, but he had asked for some time, which to my ears, sounded like he was breaking up with me.

I swallowed the sadness clogging my throat and followed our family and friends, leaving Artan behind. He would catch up with us eventually, though I hoped he didn't. Drunk the way he was, he was certain to be the first injured if it came down to a fight.

The sun was almost gone as we trailed to the western border. Lamps lighted the streets, but their glow was faint.

As Leander had told us, the alchemist group—I counted to twenty, then stopped—stood a few yards beyond the magical line protecting the enclave, away from the lights.

Theron halted right before the border line. "What do you want?"

An alchemist stepped forward. Like all the others, he wore pitch black clothes. His skin was pale, his eyes were black, with only a little white, and his head was bald. Underneath the mask covering the lower half of his face, there were creepy, black lips.

The alchemist twirled the shadow sword in his hands. "I thought that was an obvious answer," he said, his deep voice muffled by the mask. "We want your blood."

The alchemists formed a long line beside him, all of them sporting their shadow swords.

I channeled my magic, calling my fire. "The magic should hold, right?" I asked my grandmother, even though she had said twice in the last few minutes that it would.

Eyes on the alchemists, she nodded. "It should."

Footsteps sounded behind us, and Leander and Lash and another dozen warriors joined us, ready to defend our enclave if necessary.

"What are our orders?" Leander asked Theron.

"Nothing for now," Theron answered. "We just observe."

My mother shook her head. "This feels odd."

"I know," my father said.

"Don't do anything stupid," Theron said to our group in a low voice. "They can't attack us in here."

"If they can't attack us ..." Artan drawled. I hadn't even seen him beside us. I thought he had tripped on the way here and slept wherever he fell. With a smug grin, he threw his hands out and blew a strong wind toward the alchemists.

"Artan, stop!" I cried.

Theron grunted at him, and the others told him to stop too.

But Artan laughed as he intensified the wind, making the alchemists put their arms up and cover their faces. Some even wobbled on their feet, trying to stay upright.

Finally, Kane held Artan's hands and pushed them down.

The wind died out, but Artan turned a deadly glare to Kane. "You're dead."

Kane stepped forward, daring him. "I want to see you try."

Theron pushed them both apart. "What the hell? This is *not* the time."

After a low growl, Kane stepped back. He turned his attention back to the alchemists, but Artan kept thrashing against Theron, as if trying to get around him and get to Kane.

By Saint Sara-la-Kali, when would this end?

Thankfully, two warriors joined Theron and took over the duty of babysitting Artan, and Theron was able to stand in line with us.

As if waiting for the right moment, the alchemist who had goaded us before stepped a few steps forward. "It has been a pleasure," he said. Then, he dropped a vial on the ground. The vial broke instantly, and thick, green smoke rose to the sky, enveloping them.

"What's going on?" Ellie asked, her voice trembling, showing how nervous she was. Theron had been training with her, teaching her to defend herself, but she was the only human in our group and an easy target.

"I don't know," Sheila said. My grandmother narrowed her eyes, trying to get a better look.

"Oh, please," Artan snarled, pushing aside the two warriors watching over him. He threw his hands forward again, and his wind power washed away the green smoke.

The alchemists were gone.

"What the fuck?" Kane asked, glancing around.

Artan stumbled forward, past the border. "Let's see."

"Artan, no!" Theron snapped.

Like a stubborn child, or a grumpy drunk, Artan marched

to the area where the alchemists had occupied. He looked around, stumbling over his feet, then shrugged. "They aren't here."

My mother glanced at me. "What was that, then?"

A scream ripped through the enclave. My stomach sank.

"No," I whispered.

Our group took off toward the enclave, our desperation increasing with each step we took. More screams joined the first one, and soon we encountered tziganes fleeing through the streets.

I wanted to stop and ask what was going on, but I knew I would soon find out with my own eyes.

Before we reached the main square, we saw them.

Red alchemists and revenants swarmed through the streets.

"It was a distraction," I muttered, feeling disappointed with myself. Those alchemists who had gotten our attention at the border were probably red alchemists disguised, trying to steer us away, while they broke through a weak point.

Theron halted at the edge of the main square. "Ellie, Marisa, Dolan, and Sheila. Help rescuing the tziganes caught in this mess. The rest of us ... let's kill them all."

In a flash, my mother, father, grandmother, and best friend were gone, whisking tziganes cowering in the corners away. Theron and the others charged forward, taking out any red alchemists or revenants in their way.

I called my fire. It warmed my veins, heated my blood. Holding on to this rage, I joined the fray.

A revenant lunged at me. I twisted out of the way, but grabbed its arm. I sent my fire into it. Orange erupted from its grayish skin, burning it from the inside. The shriek that followed pierced in my ears.

I winced with the sudden pain.

Then, a red alchemist brandished his shadow sword at my head. Leaning back, I dodged the strike. I opened my hand and a ball of fire showed up in my palm. When the alchemist tried cutting me down again, I threw the fireball at his chest. The ball exploded against him, and the fire spread through his body, taking him inch by inch.

I watched as he writhed, falling on the ground like a crispy leaf.

Nobody messed with my people. Nobody.

"Oh, my dear Mirella."

Her voice cut through the grunts and yells and sword clashing sounds echoing through the main square. For a moment, all the fighting ceased, and we gawked at the young woman standing on top of the fountain's stone ledge.

Damara smiled at me, as if we were two long lost friends. Her long, brown hair billowed behind her back, like the skirt of her red dress. "It's so good to see you."

My temper rose and I clenched my hands into fists. "I knew this attack was on you, but I wasn't sure you were going to show up."

She tilted her head at me. "And miss the fun? No way." She cackled. "Speaking of fun, I expected more magic imbued at the enclave's perimeter. Breaking it wasn't fun at all."

So she had been the one to break it and help the red alchemists and revenants in. If there was a person I would have guessed could break it, it would have been Damara, but at the same time, I hadn't expected her to come looking for us.

Not yet.

I glanced around the square. Tziganes ran past, screaming. Windows and doors had been broken down. Fire engulfed the school, filling the air with heavy smoke, and the night sky with an orange glow.

We hadn't been ready.

Perhaps I could fix it. Perhaps this was my chance to end this once and for all.

"Fight me," I said, taking a step toward her. "Let the others leave. Fight me."

"Mirella, no!" Kane's voice rang louder than any other protest echoing through the square.

Ignoring him, Damara smiled at me. "And what should I expect from it?"

"If you win, you can have me." I took another step closer. "You can steal my powers, kill me, do whatever you want, as long as you leave the others alone." She seemed to consider it. "But if I win, then you surrender. Your alchemists and revenants will surrender too."

Kane appeared by my side. "Are you crazy?" He reached for my arm. "No!"

My gaze on Damara, I jerked free of him, and advanced. "What do you say?"

Damara narrowed her eyes at me. "As tempting as that sounds, I'm afraid I can't accept your offer."

"Why—?"

My question was cut short when Damara threw a few fire daggers at me. I stepped to the side, trying to avoid them, but I wasn't fast enough. But Kane was. He hooked his arm on mine and pulled me several feet away. The fire daggers licked the air behind my back, a few inches from my hair.

In a heartbeat, I realized I was in Kane's arms, his big hands around my shoulders, my hands on his chest. He looked down at me, his mouth a few inches from mine.

But that heartbeat passed and I stepped back.

I whipped toward Damara, hands raised to counter attack any more of her strikes, but she was gone.

I searched for her, but all I saw was the fighting, which had resumed, the desperate tziganes, and the fire spreading from the school to the infirmary.

My heart squeezed.

A few feet from me, a red alchemist fell to the ground. Bloody sword in hand, Theron stood behind him. He lifted his eyes to mine. "It's your call."

I knew what he meant. The enclave was swarming with our enemies, fire was spreading, and we were overrun.

I let out a long breath. "Let's go."

He nodded once. "Retreat," he called.

Our friends shifted their fights back, so they could approach us. Once we were all together, I brought up a wall of fire, blocking the revenants and red alchemists' path.

"Time to leave the enclave," I said, my heart heavy with guilt and sorrow.

3

AS WE GATHERED WHAT WAS LEFT OF OUR PEOPLE, AND FILED out of the enclave, we encountered a few more red alchemists and revenants. Most of the time, the warriors dealt with them, but when they were too many, I blocked their way with a wall of fire. Felix and Vira were able to get out too, and found us as we fled.

I felt like a coward for abandoning our home—and the tziganes we couldn't save—but if we had stayed and fought, more of us would have been hurt. Or worse, perished.

In the middle of the night, we trekked through the forest, putting as much distance as we could between us and our enemies. At every corner, after every snapping twig, at every gentle breeze, my heart hammered in my chest, sure Damara would take me by surprise.

It was early morning, and the sun was already hiking up in the sky when we found a clearing along a river coasting a steep hill and I finally relaxed, allowing everyone to stop.

In our rush to get out, we hadn't brought much, but Theron had already taken charge and was planning a trip to the nearest town to buy supplies. For now, he had sent a few warriors to check on Ramon and his pack, since they should be camped nearby.

The rest of the tziganes spread out in the clearing, sitting down on the ground. Feeling guiltier than ever, I took a seat beside my family in the center of the clearing.

Hushes, whispers, and cries reached my ears. I wanted to close my eyes and ignored it all, but I couldn't because I was hurting as much as they were. We had lost our home, we had left friends and family behind, we were tired, and starving, and sleep deprived.

My mother put an arm around my shoulders. "It'll be okay. You've done all you could. We all have."

"I'm not so sure," I whispered, though that was a stupid answer. What else could I have done? Other than killing Damara when I had the chance, I didn't know.

Ryane, Cora, and Ellie walked around the clearing, handing berries they had found nearby to the tziganes. I frowned, a little jealous of their initiative. I should have done that. I should have stepped up and come up with a plan, and made sure everyone was all right, even when they weren't.

But the numbness inside me was too great, and I could barely raise a finger, much less think straight and help others.

A couple of hours passed, and Theron came back with Kane and a few warriors, all of them with their arms loaded with tents, bedrolls, blankets, and supplies.

Once more, Theron took charge and organized tasks. The warriors put up the tents for everyone, while the younger and able women distributed the food and drinks they brought. Meanwhile, Ryane and the other healers went around the clearing, making sure the sick were okay, and that no one was injured too badly.

In no time, the brown and gray tents covered most of the clearing. A larger dark green one was placed in the center.

"Come on," Theron said, tugging my arm.

I let him carry me to inside the thick tent, where the others stood in a circle. My mother, my father, my grandmother, Ellie, Cora, Rye, Ryane, Tomas, Leander, Lash, and Kane.

"Here's the list," Leander said, passing a piece of paper to Theron.

I leaned into my half-brother, spying the list. Names. There were many names on the list. "These are the people missing?" Theron asked.

Leander nodded. "Yes."

My stomach turned as I read the names. I was relieved over not finding any of my closest friends on the list. But that didn't change the fact that someone's friends or family were.

"Do we know if they were left behind, or if they are ... dead?" I asked.

Artan glared at me. "Does it make a difference? Tziganes were left behind with revenants and alchemists. They are as good as dead." His voice was strong, unwavering. He was sober right now.

I looked down, ashamed of my question. Of everything. I wished a hole would open up in the ground and swallow me whole.

There were days when being the damn precious heart maiden was too hard.

"We should be more practical and avoid bickering," Theron said.

He was right. As the heart maiden, I had to push my feelings aside and focus. Right now, the tziganes needed me.

I inhaled a sharp breath. "We should send some scouts

back to the enclave," I suggested. "To check on how destroyed our home is, where and how the survivors are, and to see what Damara wants with Lovell."

Kane crossed his arms. "That's risky, but I agree, it needs to be done."

I glanced at him, suddenly satisfied that he was agreeing with me, but he was looking at Theron, not me.

Theron nodded. "I'll pick a few of our best warriors."

"We need to think of food and drink supplies, and a patrol rotation," I added. "Since we don't know how long we're going to stay here, we better make ourselves comfortable."

Artan snorted. "Comfortable?" He brought up a silver flask to his lips. He was already drinking again? "You think we want to get comfortable here?"

I clenched my fists. "Of course not! But you know what I meant."

"You don't need to explain yourself to him, Mirella," Kane said through gritted teeth. This time, his murderous gaze was fixed on Artan.

Artan licked his lips and smiled at Kane. "The warrior rescuing the princess. Typical."

Kane took a step forward. "What—?"

I grabbed Kane's arm and held him back. "Stop. He's not worth it."

Theron had already stepped between the two of them. He turned to Artan. "Stop making an ass of yourself," he said in a low voice.

"What?" Artan pretended to be offended. "I thought you were my friend. Shouldn't you be defending me too?"

"This is me being your friend." Theron ripped the silver flask from Artan's hands. "Stay quiet or I'll kick your ass."

Artan opened his mouth to protest, but Theron glared at him. The drunk warrior's shoulders sagged, and he grumbled under his breath.

My mother cleared her throat. "I'll take care of feeding us."

"We have injured people," I said, resuming the organization plan. "Ryane, I saw you already helped a lot of people. Can you please continue working on that?"

The young woman nodded. "Of course."

"I'll help," Ellie offered.

"Good." I turned to Theron. "We should set up security. Here, out in the open, we're more vulnerable than ever."

"I know," he said with a long sigh. "I—"

The flaps of the tent pushed aside and Rick rushed into the tent.

"Rick!" Kane said, taking him in. It was hard to miss the blood on his neck and shoulders, and the rips on his uniform. "What happened?"

"I-I just made it out of there," the warrior said, his voice trembling. "Damara broke into the house and got ahold of the former elder council members."

I held my breath. My mother gasped. Ryane put a trembling hand over her open mouth. Tension rippled through the tent.

"What did she do to them?" Artan asked, his voice suddenly devoid of all intoxication.

"She used her magic on them and turned them into some sort of mind-slaves," Rick said. Did he mean like the undead Damara had once tried to use as an army? "They attacked Joel and me, and the other tziganes who were still hiding in the enclave."

By Saint Sara-la-Kali. "Where's Joel? And the other tziganes?"

"Joel is dead. The other tziganes ... I don't know. I saw them being rounded up." Rick's eyes shone with tears. "I wanted to help, but I couldn't. I was just one against too many of them."

Theron put a firm hand over Rick's shoulders. "You did well. You're back here, safe, and you have told us a useful piece of information. You did well."

Rick nodded, trying to keep his composure.

"You must be tired," I said, keeping my voice gentle. He was hurt too. "Why don't you go with Ryane and Ellie?" I gestured for the girls to step forward. "They will show you where to rest and find something for you to drink."

Ryane grabbed Rick's arm and steered him to the tent's entrance. "Come on. We'll take care of you." Ellie and Tomas followed them out. I hoped they dressed Rick's wounds and gave him some healing tea.

What damn tea? We barely had any water.

When Rick was gone with our friends, Artan pointed a finger at me, then at Kane. "This is all the doing of your friend, Trina. She betrayed us. She brought Damara right to us."

I pressed my mouth tight before I snapped at him.

Kane didn't have the same restrains. "Trina wasn't our friend."

"No, she was your wife," Artan said, venom dripping from his words. "Who says you're not behind all of this too? You'll slit our throats while we sleep."

"Artan!" I cried, as rage rolled in waves inside me. He was being so childish, so rude.

How in the world did I love him before? Right now, I hated him.

"Artan, stop," Theron warned.

"What?" Artan turned to my brother. "Don't you think that's strange? They both came to us practically together. Trina showed her claws first, but I'm sure Kane will be the next one." He bared his teeth at Kane. "He even has the stupid heart maiden wrapped around his finger."

The only warning we got was Kane's low growl. Then, he was on Artan, punching his face. Artan's face whipped to the side with the impact, but as Kane pulled back his arm to land another strike, Artan sent a wave of wind, and pushed all of us back. The tent filled with air and the stakes shook.

"Stop!" I cried, ready to create a fire wall to separate them.

But Artan charged into Kane while we fought his wind. He landed a nasty punch on Kane's chin. Kane didn't leave it there. His eyes turning orange, he punched Artan in the stomach.

The punches flew for a few seconds, while we tried to be more than spectators.

Kane landed an elbow strike on Artan's head, sending him sprawling on the floor. The wind died and we could finally move. They were a few feet from each other, and now was my chance to create the fire wall.

But before I could do that, the men interfered. My father, Theron, Rye, Leander, and Lash held them both back, away from each other.

Kane stopped fighting at once, but Artan kept thrashing against the ones holding him.

"Artan, stop!" Theron shouted. "I'm telling you to stop before I tie you up and let you rot!"

Artan spat on the ground near Theron's boots, but he did quit. He couldn't stop glaring at Kane and me, though.

"You two are acting like children," my father spoke up. "As council members, you two are banned from meetings until you learn how to behave."

Kane wiped the blood from his lips with the back of his hand. "Fine by me." Without looking back, he marched out of the tent.

I took a step toward him, then hesitated.

"Go," Theron told me in a low voice. "The meeting is done for now anyway."

"Thank you," I muttered before sprinting after Kane.

Outside, the tziganes had quiet down. It was the middle of the night, and most tents were up. Everyone had retreated and were hopefully asleep, though a few warriors patrolled the area, to make sure we were all okay.

Kane marched by the tents. I wanted to call to him, but was afraid of waking up anyone; I kept my mouth shut. Finally, a few yards from the tents, Kane sat on a rock at the edge of the stream.

Holding my breath, I approached him.

"You shouldn't be here," he said, his gaze on the water at his side.

"I want to make sure you're okay."

His hard eyes found me. "I'm okay. You can go now."

I cast a small flame in my palm and brought it closer to him. Kane squinted against the brightness, but didn't turn away. There was a cut on his lip, and a darkening red mark on his chin and jaw.

I let go of the flame—it hovered beside us—and ripped the sleeve of my blouse. Then, I knelt beside the stream, dunked the fabric in the water, and twisted it to wring out the excess.

Gently, I reached for Kane's face and pressed the cool fabric to his skin. "I wish I had a frozen bag of peas, but this is all I can do right now." I frowned. "Wait, that isn't true." I let go of the fabric and placed both my hands on his face. I called my fire and sent it him, filling my mind with healing thoughts. Slowly, the red marks disappeared and the cut on his lip closed.

With his intense gaze locked on mine, Kane reached up and wrapped his fingers around my wrist. My breath caught. But instead of pulling me to him as I wished, Kane pushed my hands away.

"I don't need your help," he said, his voice low.

My heart squeezed. "Kane ..."

"No." He shook his head. "Don't Kane me. I really don't want to talk about ... anything right now."

I swallowed the hurt and my pride. "You can't ignore me forever."

"You're the heart maiden. Nobody can ignore you forever."

I flinched. What was he saying? That the only reason he was enduring me right now was because I was the heart maiden?

"I want to snap at you right now," I confessed. "I want to tell you that even though I am the heart maiden, you don't have to deal with me. You can even pretend that I don't exist, if that's your wish ... but I can't. I can't because I don't want you to ignore me." I clasped my hands behind my back before I lost control over them and I reached for him again. "I want quite the opposite, actually."

With a heavy sigh, Kane pushed to his feet. Looming over

me, he said, "We're not having this conversation. Not yet." He walked away.

"Kane." His name flew from my mouth before I could stop myself. Kane halted, but he didn't turn. "I'm sorry, Kane. If I could, I would go back in time and undo it all. I would never have allowed that to happen. And you would be by my side right now."

Kane didn't move for a moment, and I didn't dare to breathe.

Despite my wishes and prayers, Kane resumed walking and left me alone by the stream. I sank down on the rock he had been seated on, as tears filled my eyes.

I loved him with all my heart and soul, but I had no idea how I could prove that to him.

OVER THE NEXT COUPLE OF DAYS, OUR CAMP GREW. BIGGER tents had been set up and served as kitchen, cafeteria, infirmary, and school—not that the kids were actually having classes at a time like this, but we needed a place to keep and entertain them. Felix and Vira settled outside the camp, beside a thick, low tree, near the stream.

Ryane and Ellie and some other tziganes had treated the injured and sick, and they all were on the mend. My mother and my grandmother spent most of the day cooking for the entire camp—thankfully a lot of others helped, making it easier on them. Wanting to do more, Cora and Rye had joined the warriors in the patrol rounds. Artan had become a useless drunk who rarely left his tent, and when he did, he bitched about everything.

Meanwhile, the council and I had meetings whenever we could, trying to figure out what to do. Our spies came and went, telling us that Damara and her army hadn't moved from Lovell yet.

And they hadn't spotted Trina.

That was a mystery to me. She had clearly been at Damara's side when they attacked the den of Ramon's pack, but she hadn't been beside Damara when she attacked the enclave. Had I been imagining things? If yes, then where was Trina? Had she been caught? Killed? The thoughts upset me.

Since his camp wasn't far from ours, Ramon and his beta, Weston, came often to check on us. He also had a score to settle with Damara and he wanted to help us in any way he could.

On our fourth morning at our new—but temporary—camp, I was teaching dance to little girls with Ellie, when a sudden pain burned inside my chest, taking my breath away.

I was in the middle of a pirouette and the intensity of the pain brought me to my knees.

Ellie stared at me, shocked. "What happened?"

The pain came back and I gritted my teeth, locking the scream rising to my throat. "I lost my balance," I said simply, not wanting to let the kids know the truth.

Ellie narrowed her eyes at me, clearly not convinced. She extended a hand to me and helped me up. "You're practically a professional," she whispered. "You wouldn't lose your balance on a simple pirouette."

The pain came back and I involuntarily squeezed her hand. She yelped. "Mirella?"

"It's nothing," I lied. Then, I shook my head. "Actually, I don't know. Keep the class going. I'm going to find Sheila."

She held on to my hand firmer. "Want me to come with you?"

The girls, all ranging from four to ten years old, swarmed around us, asking what the next step was to our little improvised dance.

I smiled at them, though my insides were screaming. "I

have a meeting right now, girls, so Ellie is going to take over, okay? I'll be back as soon as I can."

I squeezed Ellie's hand one more time. She nodded at me, then smiled at the little girls. "Come on, girls. Let's keep this party going." Letting go of my hand, she turned to the girls.

I rushed out of the tent, before the pain came back and I collapsed in front of them.

Some tziganes were in the streets the tents had created. They greeted me as I speed-walked past them, their faces grim with pain and grief. I weaved through the tents, aiming for the camp's center, where the council's tent was located. Even if there wasn't an active meeting now, I was sure I would find someone in there.

I was a few yards from the tent, when the pain rolled back inside me. My chest constricted and burned, and I crouched down, trying to breathe through the pain and not scream.

This time, when the pain reared back, another sensation was left behind.

A tug.

A call.

The heart flower's song, but a little different. Stronger, hotter, more aggressive.

With a hand pressed to my chest, I stood and glanced around. The scent of smoke and wildflowers overwhelmed me, making me dizzy.

Shit, I had to follow this call. Right now.

I took a step forward and Kane appeared right before me.

"I feel something," he said, his voice rough. Hazel eyes round, he stared at my hand against my chest. "That." He pointed to my hand, then rested his over his chest. "I feel it. A call of sorts."

I blinked at him. "What? Why?"

"Could it be the heart flower?" He shook his head, discarding the idea. "That's absurd. Only the heart maiden can hear the heart flower's song."

"Is it burning you on the inside, like a fire that rolls inside you and then leaves you with a forward tugging?" I asked. "Can you smell the scent of fire burning and flowers?"

He nodded. "I don't understand."

Me neither.

From the east, Theron and Ramon walked toward the council's tent. My brothers saw Kane and me and approached us.

"You two don't look too good," Ramon said, in a teasing tone.

"There's something going on," I said.

Ramon lost the amused expression and straightened. "What happened?"

I glanced around, not wanting to talk about whatever this was in public, afraid of creating rumors or misplaced panic.

"Let's get inside," Theron suggested.

The four of us entered the tent. It now had a thin, wooden table in the middle and several folding chairs around it. Every time I came in here, I thought of the legend of King Arthur and the round table. Only, our table was rectangular.

As expected, there were people inside the tent. My mother, my father, and my grandmother. They were checking a long grocery list before going on a store run.

My mother saw us first and smiled at me. "Hi, Mi—"

Her voice died when the pain came back, bringing fire and agony to my veins. I would have fallen on the ground if Ramon hadn't caught me. Beside me, Kane groaned, his fist pounding against his chest.

"What's happening?" Dolan asked, rushing for me.

I was helped to a chair. My mother and Sheila occupied the chairs beside me, while my father hovered over me. Across the table, Kane sat down too.

His eyes met mine.

What was going on?

The pain retreated and I inhaled deeply. The tug was still there, though, just as strong as before.

"All right, what's happening?" Theron asked.

"We don't know," Kane said.

"It feels like a heart flower calling, but it's different," I said.

Ramon frowned. "Are you feeling this too, Kane?"

Kane rubbed at his chest. "I have no idea how the heart flower's song is supposed to be, but I'm sure feeling something."

"The two of you feeling this same call," Theron muttered. "That is suspicious. Could it be a trick from Damara and her alchemists? Like a spell to bring you both to her?"

"What would she want with me?" Kane asked.

Theron shrugged. "You've been by Mirella's side since you first showed up here. She might want to kill you out of spite."

I winced. Kane frowned.

"We should send out more spies to check on them," Ramon said. "If Damara is plotting something big, we'll find out. I can get a few of my wolves to go."

"That's a good idea," Theron said.

Ramon was ready to walk out of the tent, when Sheila spoke up. "Actually, I think I know what this is."

Everyone turned to my grandmother.

"*Puri daj*, what do you mean?" Ramon asked.

"To be honest, I'm a little confused about it, but I'll tell you what I know," she started. "There was a legend we told each other long ago, and it was about the fire flower. It's supposed to be a version of a heart flower that's tremendously powerful. Legend said it was the strongest thing a heart maiden could find, although no one had seen one in centuries."

"So, it's a legend?" Dolan asked.

"I thought so, but now I'm not so sure," Sheila said.

"And how do you know this is the fire flower?" I asked.

My grandmother shook her head. "I don't. I'm just taking a guess here, since you said it's like the heart flower's song but stronger."

Fire flower.

The tug was like a fire rope, and I could smell smoke in the air.

That had to be it.

"The heart flower is already powerful," Theron said. "What does a fire flower do?"

"I don't know," Sheila admitted. "But if it really is as powerful as legend says, it might be what we need to defeat Damara. If Mirella can absorb its powers, she'll definitely win against Damara."

"Then we need to find this flower," Ramon said.

"But it's a myth," Theron argued.

"They are feeling the call." Ramon pointed to Kane and me. "It's not a myth."

"What about me?" Kane asked. "Why am I also feeling it?"

"I don't know," Sheila said again.

My mother glanced at Kane, then at me. "You should go find it. Both of you. If there's such flower, you take it and use it. If there isn't, then you come back. Meanwhile, we'll be working on a plan to take down Damara and her army."

I stared at my mother, shocked by her words.

"I agree," Theron said.

"Me too," Dolan said.

Ramon raised his hand, as if adding up to a vote. "Me three."

My grandmother reached to me and patted my hand. "Go. Hopefully, you'll bring back a miracle."

A new wave of pain started deep inside me. I hunched my back, bracing for it. Gritting my teeth, I endured as the fire burned inside me.

Once more, the pain faded and I was able to breathe easily again. But the call was still there. Strong and relentless.

Across from the table, Kane watched me. From the sweat beading his forehead and his splayed hand on the table, I was sure he had experienced the same pain I did. Even if this was the mythical fire flower, why was he being assaulted by the same pain? Why was he feeling the flower's call?

"What do you think?" I asked, my voice weak.

He nodded at me. "Let's go."

5

———

AFTER CHANGING INTO THE WARRIOR'S UNIFORM, PACKING A BAG with extra clothes and some food, and even two bedrolls—since we had no idea how far this flower was and how long we would take to get there—Kane and I left the camp.

At first, we had thought about going with a group, for safety, but we soon decided against it. One, having a larger group might slow us down, and two, I would feel better knowing the warriors were protecting the camp right now.

It wasn't even noon yet, but we had no time to waste. I could only hope we found this flower soon and were back by sundown.

All wishful thinking.

After hours hiking through the forest and enduring several waves of pain, Kane and I didn't seem to be any closer to the damn flower.

Adding to the pain and the call, the air around us was tense. Charged. Bag over his shoulders and swords secured on his back, Kane had barely looked my way for the hours we had been walking—together and alone.

Wouldn't this be a great opportunity for us to make up? At first, after I ignored the pain that burned like liquid fire, I had been excited about this trip. He would be forced to talk to me, to watch out for me, to plan with me.

And yet, it was like I wasn't even there.

I had tried starting a conversation a few times.

"Does it hurt a lot?"

"Do you believe in this myth?"

"What do you think the flower does?

After a bout of pain, I asked, "Are you okay?"

But he only gave me short, harsh answers, cutting me off completely.

I ended up giving up.

The sun set and we kept going, despite the soreness in my legs and the rounds of pain that drained my energy. Wasn't he feeling tired too? Didn't he plan on stopping and resting? Since I had already tried talking to him and he had barely grunted at me, I didn't say anything this time. I conjured a couple of flames and sent them hovering around us, illuminating our path while we walked through the dark forest.

Finally, it was past midnight when Kane relented. He slowed down and glanced around a space between a few thick trees and bushes. "I guess we need to camp here."

Without looking at me, he put down his bag, unrolled the two bedrolls, and walked away again.

Confused, I sat down on one of the bedrolls. I rummaged through my bag until I found my wrapped ham and cheese sandwich. I wasn't hungry, but I forced myself to nibble on it as much as I could, because I would need my stamina to keep going.

I tried keeping my mind clear, if only for a moment, and focused on my surroundings. It was mostly quiet here. I could hear a few insects and small animals, the gentle breeze ruffling the leaves, and the faint rush of a river nearby.

A few minutes later, Kane came back with his arms full of firewood. He dropped the branches a few feet from the bedrolls, forming a small pile. Then, he grabbed a lighter from his bag.

Before he could light the fire, I snapped my fingers and flames sparked to life in the improvised campfire.

"*Nais tuke*," he muttered, putting the lighter away. He dropped back on the bedroll beside mine and picked up some of his food.

The silence, the tension ... it was killing me.

But I didn't know what to say anymore. I had already said everything. That I was sorry, that it never should have happened, that I wanted to erase it from my past, from my mind.

It didn't matter. The hurt Kane felt blocked anything else.

His marriage had been arranged, but as a proud tzigane, Kane wanted to honor his bride. He tried to love her; he wanted to. He dedicated himself to her. And as far as I know, she did too. But Trina wasn't satisfied. She ended up cheating on Kane—sleeping with some other guy. Because he had trusted her, because he believed their relationship could have worked, that betrayal broke Kane. It broke his heart.

And then when he finally accepted love again, when he actually fell for someone, that someone broke his trust by kissing some other guy.

I did that to him.

I couldn't really blame him for hating me right now.

The pain started anew, and I almost choked on the last bite of my sandwich. I leaned forward, trying to brace myself until the burning sensation traveled down my body, and I could breathe again.

I glanced at the man a few feet to my side, and he had his eyes shut tight, his lips pressed together, and his hands clenched.

The pain was gone faster this time, but the pull was stronger. I hoped that meant we were closer to this damn fabled flower.

"I'm sorry this is happening to you," I whispered, staring at the fire.

"It's not your fault," he said, his voice curt.

"If it really is the fire flower, it might be."

"Well ..." He sighed. "If you were supposed to feel both our pains alone, I'm glad it's split in half and I have to deal with it."

I looked at him. His hazel eyes shone with the flames' dance, intense as usual. I wanted to ask him what he meant, but I was afraid he would shut me down again and go back to ignoring me.

Besides, I really couldn't imagine feeling twice as much pain. "When you put it that way, then I'm glad too."

Kane cleared his throat and averted his eyes. "We should rest." He cleaned up his dinner and lay down on the bedroll, his back turned to me. "If you can, just dim the fire."

Without moving a muscle, I willed the flames to dull a little.

Then, I stared at Kane's back.

Saint Sara-la-Kali, I needed some help. I was sure Kane was the one for me. I was sure I loved him with all my heart and soul. But how could I gain his trust again? How could I make him forgive me and forget what happened?

Sighing, I lay down on my bedroll, but sleep didn't come.

Instead, my mind raced and my heart hurt with all that had happened since I became the heart maiden. I had lost friends, seen the enclave destroyed and taken more than once, been imprisoned and tortured, and had my heart broken and healed again. I had found a warm family, made peace with my mother, and found true love.

A true love who wasn't speaking to me right now.

Restless, I climbed out of the bedroll and tiptoed away from our camp. I followed the sound of the river. As I suspected, the river wasn't even a hundred yards from the camp. Here, the narrow patch cut through the forest, but ran fast, its waters wild. The crescent moon shone down, giving it a magical glow.

I crouched by its bank and dipped my fingers in the cold water.

Sometimes I felt so tired, so hopeless. I felt like I was the worst heart maiden in the world. If only there was a way I could pass on the mantle, I would. To whom? I didn't know, but I was sure there was a badass female tzigane out there who could do a much better job than me.

A silver spark in the middle of the river caught my eye. I leaned forward, trying to see what it was, glittering from a couple of feet under the water. The silver spot shone brighter, and I stepped into the river, trying to reach it. After two steps, I stretched my arm and—

Pain shot through my veins, a burning sensation that made me double over.

My foot slid on the slippery rocky bottom, and I fell into the river. The cold water doused the worst of the pain, but by then I was already being carried down the river by the strong current. Panic threatened to break free while I moved my arms, trying to swim. But I couldn't do much against such a strong river. I mostly focused on taking big gulps of air whenever my head emerged from the water.

I slammed against rocks, scratching my arms. I tried holding on to them, but they were too slippery. Exhaustion joined the panic swirling inside me. It was getting harder and harder to keep my head above water, to fight the current, to breathe.

If I didn't stop soon—

I threw out my arm, trying to grab hold of the rock I had slammed into, but ended up closing my hand around a thick branch that had grown above the water's surface. Grunting, I pulled myself out of the water, and to the bank of the river.

I lay on the rocky shore, breathing hard.

By Saint Sara-la-Kali. I had to get up. I had to go back to camp before Kane woke up and didn't find me there. I had to rest. I was so damned tired. Eyes closed, I pressed my cheek against the rocks. I could sleep here, if I let myself.

I didn't think I could stop it either.

A warm light shone behind my eyelids and my eyes shot open.

"Well, well, what do we have here?"

A group of alchemists formed a semicircle around me.

I jumped to my feet—swaying to the side on my wobbly feet—and called my magic. "Stay back!" I warned, my feet already back in the water.

The alchemist holding the lantern laughed. "What will you do if we don't, heart maiden?"

I gulped, trying to take everything in at once. There were nine alchemists in front of me. A wooden cabin stood a few yards behind them, lights shining from inside. There could be more alchemists in there. Tired and hurt against nine or possibly more alchemists? The odds weren't good.

Even so, it wasn't like I would give up without a fight. I held on to my fire. "You won't live to regret it."

The alchemist laughed, the sound distorted because of his mask. "That was funny." His dark gaze hardened as he extended his free hand and the shadow sword appeared. "Get her!"

The other alchemists called their swords and rushed me.

6

I BROUGHT UP A FIRE WALL BETWEEN THE ALCHEMISTS AND ME, caging me against the raging river. I glanced back at the water, imagining if I could try to cross it without slipping and being carried down the river again.

It was either braving the fast waters or the dark alchemists.

There wasn't a good solution here.

I felt my energy draining as I held up the shield while the alchemists tried to break it. My hands shook and I knelt in the shallow water, trying to save my stamina.

Then, two alchemists jumped from behind me.

I yelled in surprise, and lost the hold on my fire wall. The alchemists held my arms and pushed me forward. Once the shield was gone, the others advanced.

The alchemist from before passed the lantern to another one, then halted one foot from me. "Enough playing." He closed black iron-like cuffs around my wrists.

The hell ... I channeled my magic, intent on melting these damn cuffs and blasting them all with my fire, but my magic flickered and didn't hold on. "W-what is this?" I asked without meaning to.

The alchemist pulled off his mask and smiled at me with his black lips. "Like our special binds?"

I tried again. I furrowed my brows and focused, calling my fire. Once more, it sparked a few times, then faded away like smoke in the wind.

I stared at the alchemist in horror. "What did you do?"

"Wouldn't you like to know." He snapped his fingers. "Take her inside."

The other alchemists pushed me forward. I tripped over my feet and almost face-planted on the rocky ground. Their firm hands around my upper arms kept me upright while they dragged me toward the cabin.

My panic increased. What were they going to do with me? Kill me and drain me of my blood? Were they regular alchemists, or were they with Damara? Would they hand me over to her?

I felt as if, when I entered that cabin, it was all over.

I let out a loud cry and jerked against the alchemists holding me. At first, they let go of me, but in my exhausted state, I wasn't able to take one step before I lost my footing and almost fell. The alchemists got me again, holding firmer this time, hurting me.

"Be a nice girl or we'll kill you," one of them whispered in my ear.

I shuddered in disgust and fear.

The damn pain from whatever that call was hit me again. It was too much. I couldn't handle it. I cried again as the burning pain consumed me. My legs melted from under me, my head spun, my vision darkened.

I was going to faint and these alchemists would kill me.

This was it. If I closed my eyes, I wouldn't ever open them again.

"Mirella!"

Hearing Kane's voice was like an instant freshener. The pain was gone, my head cleared, and even though I couldn't call my magic, I regained my footing and pushed against the alchemists holding me.

"What the hell?" an alchemist yelled. "Kill him!"

I kept being dragged toward the cabin as the sound of swords clashing and grunts reached my ears. I tried fighting harder, getting free of them. I also tried glancing back to have an idea of what was going on, but other than knowing Kane was fighting the alchemists, I couldn't see anything.

Then, I was on the porch of the cabin. The door was opening.

My gut twisted. No, no, no.

Trying a new tactic, I faked tripping and crouched down, throwing the alchemists off-balance. When their grips loosened, I threw myself back and did a backward roll. I ended up falling off the two porch steps, while the alchemists stared at me, a little slow on the uptake. By the time they charged me, I was on my feet and turning around.

Bodies piling up at his feet, Kane brandished his twin swords left and right, cutting the alchemists like they were made of leaves. His eyes glowed orange, matching the shine of his blades.

"Kane!" I ran to him.

He swung his sword wide, slicing an alchemist's chest open. The body fell to his feet, and he turned to me. "The shackles," he said, raising his sword.

I skidded to a stop and extended my arms as far as I could. Kane dropped his sword, cutting through the link that united the cuffs. Magic cut, they opened and fell to the ground with a heavy clank.

They were gone.

My magic was back.

I called it and it answered instantly, filling my veins with my fire, its warmth welcoming and satisfying.

The two alchemists who had been holding me before lunged at me. I lifted my hands and a circle of fire surrounded them.

"What the—?" one of them shouted as he tried to cross the chest-high fire wall. It burned him and he pulled back.

Sure they wouldn't be able to get out of there until I let go of the circle, I turned to the last two of Kane's opponents. Like a beautiful fighter, Kane danced with them. He ducked under the sword, which dripped with a dark green liquid, twisting out of the way. He turned in an expected way, landing a hard elbow strike to the alchemist's ribs. The alchemist let out a howl, which was cut short when Kane twisted again, this time putting distance between him and his opponent, and swinging his sword across, slicing the alchemist's throat.

The second alchemist tried interfering, going for Kane while he was busy, but I sent a fire dart that exploded against his chest. The alchemist stumbled back. He turned his enraged gaze to me and, with a yell, charged at me.

I sent another dart at him, a more powerful one this time. The strike exploded against his stomach, and orange fire spread through his clothes. He screamed as the fire ate his clothes and burned his flesh. When it reached his chest, the magic in my fire numbed him. The alchemist fell on his face and the fire died out.

Sometimes I wondered if what I was doing was right. Should I avoid killing these evil men? They sure wouldn't hesitate to kill Kane and me and anyone else who crossed their paths. And I would let them live.

But if I killed because I could, how did that make me any better than them? I didn't want to be evil. I didn't want to kill mindlessly. I wanted to be a good, kind, just heart maiden, and if that started by stunning my enemies instead of killing them, so be it.

When all the alchemists were either dead or stunned or contained, Kane turned to me. "Are you okay?" His hands hovered over my arms, his eyes rummaged through my face, neck, and shoulders, where I probably had nasty scratches. "By Saint Sara-la-Kali, what happened?"

I took a step back, uncomfortable with his attention. He had ignored me for so long, and now he was all over me? Was it because the precious heart maiden had been almost killed? If he still hated me, it was the only reason I could think of.

"Let's get out of here," I mumbled.

I sidestepped him and headed for the river. In silence, Kane followed me.

At the riverbank, the night was clearer and brighter, so I didn't cast any flames to illuminate our way.

"If you're not too hurt, we should go faster." Walking by me with his long legs, Kane grabbed my hand and tugged me forward.

I was exhausted, hurt, and now that I thought about it, starving, but I wouldn't tell him any of that. One, because I agreed with him—we needed to get out of here. Two, because I didn't want him pampering me.

Wasn't it odd how a few hours ago I had been dying for his attention, and now that I had it, I felt like I didn't deserve it?

We made it back to our camp, grabbed our bags and

bedrolls, and set out through the forest, following the tug in our chests, and putting some distance between us and those alchemists.

Kane took the lead, weaving through the trees at a fast pace.

But the more we walked, the heavier my legs grew, the shallower my breathing became, the blurrier my vision turned.

After a while, Kane spun around and faced me. "Why didn't you tell me you're having a hard time?"

I bumped into his chest and took a large step back. "Because we need to go. We need to make sure we're far from those alchemists."

"I can deal with them if they come, but I don't think I can carry you for long if you faint." He took my bag from me. "We'll rest for a couple of hours right here."

I shook my head, but that only made me dizzier. "We should go. The sooner we find this flower, the sooner we can go back." Home. I almost said home at the end of my sentence, but there was no home to go back to. Just a crappy camp where our people were hiding.

"Mirella," he rasped, his voice tight. "Stop being stubborn." He took my bedroll and opened it right there, in the middle of the trees. "Now, lay down and rest. It's an order."

I gaped at him. "You can't order me."

"I don't care." He clasped his big hands on my shoulders and pushed me down on the bedroll.

I tried resisting, but who was I kidding? I needed the rest, and arguing with Kane would get nowhere. "Fine," I muttered as my butt hit the bedroll.

I lay down, but Kane said, "Wait." Frowning, I watched as he crouched in front of me and rummaged through his bag.

"Here." He pulled out a small bowl with a lid. A healing ointment. He unscrewed the lid, dabbed some of the white paste on his fingertip, and reached for my face. I pulled back. He groaned. "Let me do this, or I'll do it when you're sleeping."

I let out a long sigh and tried relaxing, while his fingers traced the scratches on my face, neck, and shoulders. But it was hard to relax when he was touching me with such gentleness. Despite his careful pampering, his brows were furrowed, his eyes hard, and his lips pressed as if he was still mad at me. He picked at a piece of cloth hanging from my arm. My uniform was ripped and still a little wet from my trip down the river. Thankfully, I had brought another set in my bag. But I was too tired to change now. I would do it after I rested.

The ointment stung when he applied it to a scratch on my shoulder. "By Saint Sara-la-Kali," I hissed.

"Sorry," he said in a low voice. "This is the worst one. The others won't hurt as much."

"If only I could heal myself," I muttered.

His hand froze. "Have you tried?" I shook my head. "Try it," he said, pulling his hands back.

"I'm too tired," I said. "I'm not sure I have enough strength for that."

"Just try it."

Frowning, I called my magic. It came forward, warming my veins in a pleasant way. I did what I had always done: focused on healing, on taking the pain away, on good vibes, and feeling better.

Nothing happened.

"Perhaps it only works on others." On him, actually. He was the only one I could heal. With the others, I could only soothe their pain.

"Here." Kane pushed forward, his knees right outside of mine, and took my hands in his. He turned them over, so my palms were resting in his hands, then he cupped my face. His intense gaze locked on mine, he said, "Do it now. Think about healing me, but try to redirect it to you."

"That sounds not only hard, but awkward."

"Just do it," he insisted.

I rolled my eyes, but tried it anyway. I imagined him with scratches covering his face, neck, and shoulders. My stomach tightened as I became instantly upset. I didn't like seeing him hurt. My magic flowed to him, as if he was an extension of myself. With thoughts of healing, I redirected the magic to me.

I gasped as I felt the tiny scratches itching and closing. It worked! Somehow, it had worked. One more miracle related to Kane that I couldn't explain.

Kane's eyes skimmed my face, his expression still murderous.

Once I felt all the scratches gone, I dropped my hands and leaned back a little.

But Kane didn't let go of me. Instead, his hands slid down to my shoulders. He let out a long sigh. "Do you have any idea of what I felt when I woke up and you were gone? All of your things were still there and all I could think of was that you had been taken." He shook his head. "I don't even like to remember that feeling." His hands tightened around my shoulders. "I thought ... I thought you had been killed."

"I-I'm fine," I whispered. "I'm fine now."

"Mirella ..." His gaze, always so intense, softened, and tears brimmed in his eyes. "If you had died, I couldn't bear it."

My heart skipped a beat. "Kane, you shouldn't say things

like that." I rolled my shoulders, pushing his hands away. "Don't give me false hope."

"It's not false," he said. "I was an idiot for keeping you away for so long. Deep down, I knew it didn't mean anything, that Artan was the guilty one, but I just couldn't swallow my pride. I had been hurt before, and I was trying to protect myself."

I held my breath. "What are you saying?"

"I love you, Mirella." Kane took my hands and pulled me to him. "I love you too much and I want to be with you. Forever."

A tear slid down my face. By Saint Sara-la-Kali. "I love you too."

Kane leaned over me and his lips brushed against mine. A moan ripped through my throat as relief and contentment filled my chest. I wound my arms around his neck and pulled him closer to me. Bracing us, he lowered me down on the bedroll, then eased his body over mine. I gasped, realizing I had missed even this, his body against mine, his weight pressed over me.

Kane stared at me for a moment. "I missed you," he whispered, echoing my thoughts.

"Just kiss me," I whispered, suddenly wriggling with pure desire and love.

With a sly smile, Kane lowered his head to mine. But he didn't kiss me. He teased me. His tongue ran across my lower lips, his hand inched under the thermal shirt, his fingers caressing the skin of my stomach. I arched into him, trying to kiss him for real, but he turned his head and licked my jaw, nibbled on my ear, rained kisses down my neck, sending a different kind of fire to my veins.

Desire and passion fought with the exhaustion that

claimed my muscles and my mind, and I tried enduring it for a little while longer. I needed Kane and I needed him now.

Finally, his lips found mine and Kane kissed me. He tasted of mint and coffee and chocolate, and I wanted more, more, more. The kiss started slow, but soon it deepened, as if Kane was claiming my soul, as if he wanted to imprint his mark in my heart, so we could never be apart again.

We wouldn't. By Saint Sara-la-Kali, we wouldn't.

Surprising me, Kane pulled back a little, breaking the kiss. His eyes locked on mine. "As much as I would like to keep going, I know you're tired. After all that happened tonight, we both should rest a little."

I tried not pouting. "I don't want to rest."

He chuckled. "Yes, you do." He planted a peck on my lips. "Don't worry, I intend to take good care of you later. I promise." He settled down beside me on the bedroll. "But first, we need to sleep." He pulled me closer to him, so I had my back pressed to his chest, my hips aligned with his. He snaked his hand around my waist, and buried his face on my neck. "Just like this."

"Do you think I can sleep with you like that?" All I wanted was to jump him. Damn my muscles for being so sore and tired.

He ran his lips on the nape of my neck, his warm breath sending a delicious shiver down my spine. "You better. Good night, Mi."

I groaned. "Good night, teaser."

He chuckled, but his arms only tightened around me.

Truth be told, I couldn't think of a better way to rest. Feeling happy for the first time in two weeks, I relaxed in his arms and stopped fighting the fatigue.

7

THE FIRST ORANGE AND PINK RAYS ALREADY STAINED THE SKY when Kane and I woke. We kissed once before getting up, then we were all business. We packed, ate something, and I changed my torn thermal shirt for another one. Then, we kept on with our quest: to find a mythical fire flower.

As we hiked through the forest, one thing I realized was that the tug in our chests was stronger now, but the pain that had assaulted us before was almost nonexistent. We both hadn't felt it for a few hours now, and the last time it had come, it had been milder than before, much easier to endure.

I hoped that meant we were getting close to this fire flower. I wanted to go back to our family and friends—I was worried about them. A lot of things could happen in the twenty hours we had been gone, and a lot more could happen by the time we made it back.

I tried not to hope this flower was real, but I couldn't help it. A more powerful flower than the heart flower? Was that possible? Would I really be stronger than Damara? Would I be able to defeat her? To take down her army, make them surrender, protect my people, and return them to our home?

I shook my head, pushing those thoughts—and hope—away.

Another hour passed before I noticed Kane's steps slowing.

I glanced at him, worried. "Are you okay?"

He smiled at me, but it seemed forced. "I'm fine."

I halted. "Why are you lying?"

"It's nothing."

I stepped in front of him. "Kane, tell me what's going on."

"It's just a scratch," he said, waving me off. "I'll be fine."

"A scratch?" That didn't make sense. Hadn't I sent my magic into him last night? Hadn't it healed me through him? Shouldn't it have healed him too? I reached for him. "Where?"

Hand over his stomach, he stepped back. "It's fine."

"By Saint Sara-la-Kali, do you already want another fight?" I swatted his hand away and tugged his shirt up. A nasty dark red line cut through the side of his stomach to his waist, a good four inches. It wasn't deep, but it was scabbed with blood, and a dark shadow surrounded it. I gasped. "Is this ...?"

"The liquid from the alchemists' swords. It was poison, yes."

He had changed shirts and stopped the bleeding behind my back, while being furious about me getting hurt.

I was the one furious now. "Why didn't you show it to me?" Then, I remembered the healing spell. "Why isn't it healed?"

"I think ..." He swallowed hard. Holy shit, sweat lined his forehead and drenched his shirt, and his hands were shaking.

"I think it's some kind of magical poison. You can't heal it like that."

What did he mean? "Then what am I supposed to do?"

"We should find the fire flower as soon as we can. If it's as powerful as the legend says, its magic might be able to heal me."

"But we could still be hours away from it," I said. Besides, we didn't even know if it was real. This could be a wild goose chase. A trick from Damara to send Kane and me away, so she could attack the camp or kill us without any witnesses.

With a long breath, Kane swayed to the side. I reached for him, and even though he was bigger and heavier than me, I was able to keep him upright.

He started to crouch. "Just let me catch my breath."

"No, no, no." I held on to him. I passed his arm over my shoulders and clasped his waist. If he was going to lie down and rest somewhere, it should be in a concealed place. Staying vulnerable in an open space in broad daylight was like inviting trouble. "Hang on a little longer."

Suppressing the panic rising in my chest, I walked on, half carrying Kane with me, looking for a safe place to lay him down. A few minutes later, I found a half-hidden cave at the base of a steep hill.

We paused at the entrance and I sent a ball of fire inside. The light floated in the cave, shining bright. Thankfully, the cave wasn't too big and there weren't any animals inside.

The fireball kept floating in the air, while I unrolled a bedroll at the back of the cave and helped Kane down.

I lifted his shirt again and examined his wounds. I wasn't an expert in healing and herbs, but we had to have something for this. I rummaged through my bag, then his, looking for herbs and other things we brought.

I stared at the little healing paste he had used on me before.

"I applied that earlier," he said, his voice thin. "It didn't do anything."

"There has to be something I can do," I said, despair lacing my words. "I can go around the forest, gathering herbs to create a potion to reverse the poison." I really wanted to stay and take care of him, but staying and staring at him wouldn't heal him.

"I don't think that will work since we don't know what kind of poison this is."

Well, then I would find out what kind of poison it was.

I leaned over Kane and pressed my lips to his. "Hang in there. I'll be right back."

His eyes widened and he grabbed my arm. "What are you doing?"

"I'm going to find out which poison it is," I said, pulling back. "And get an antidote."

Understanding dawned on him. "Mirella, no. You can't go back there."

"I can and I will." I grabbed water and snacks from my bag and left them beside Kane. "Drink and eat. Try to keep your strength. Stay awake. I'll be back."

"Mirella, no!"

Determined, I ignored Kane's protests as I marched out of the cave and went after the alchemists.

8

___

WITH ONE THOUGHT IN MY MIND, I RAN. HOPEFULLY, THE three alchemists we had left alive were still at that riverside cabin. If I surprised them, I was sure I could eliminate two before trapping the third one. Then, I would force him to give me the antidote.

My rage and panic were so overwhelming, I kept seeing me blast the three remaining alchemists to pieces. It would release my tension, but it would make me feel terrible after.

I shook my head. I would worry about that later. Right now, I had to find them and get the antidote.

What I had forgotten was my madness. The alchemists' cabin was definitely more than three miles away from where he was, and if I wasn't mistaken, that was the farthest I had been without succumbing to the fire heart fever.

I wasn't sure how much farther I could go, but I wasn't giving up now.

The madness didn't hit me all at once, as I expected. It came slowly. The more I walked and ran, the stronger it got.

First, it brought the shaking to my hands and arms. Next, my breathing grew shallow. Then, my sight got blurry.

No, no, I couldn't go down like this.

I took in long breaths, trying to clear my mind, to hold on. Kane depended on me. If I fell now, if the madness overtook me, he would die, and I couldn't let that happen.

Channeling my magic and hoping to gain clarity, I pushed through. I stomped through the forest and continued toward the cabin.

After a couple of hours, I arrived at the alchemists' cabin. By then, I had already collapsed twice, but had been able to recover. Although, resisting the madness felt harder with each passing second.

The bodies littering the river's edge were gone. There were no alchemists in sight, but I could see smoke coming out of the cabin's chimney. They had to be inside.

I watched the windows, trying to get a glimpse of them.

As if on cue, two alchemists walked by the window. A few minutes, later, two more crossed by.

Four so far.

Another couple of minutes passed, and I didn't see anyone else. That didn't mean there weren't twenty alchemists inside the small cabin, but I didn't have time to waste. If I couldn't deal with them normally, then I could use one thing to my advantage.

I stopped fighting and let the madness consumed me.

My veins filled with my fire and I trudged forward.

The alchemists realized I was coming for them only when I reached the front porch. One of them opened the door, shadow sword in hand, thinking he could stop me.

His mistake.

There was no sympathy in me right now. No good heart. There was only fire, power, purpose, and madness.

I barely felt it as I raised my hand and blasted him with my magic. The fire hit him like a bomb, consuming his body in mere seconds and burning him to a crisp.

The other alchemists came for me, and they met the same end—all of them, except for one, the one who had shone the lantern in my face when I ended up at the river's edge.

I enveloped him in fire, strong enough to instill fear in him, but not too seriously harm him. Not yet.

"The poison from the swords," I said, my voice deep, rough. Not my own. "Where's the antidote?"

"There's none," he said, glaring at me.

A thin trail of fire wound around his neck and squeezed. "Where's the antidote?"

The alchemist gagged, but didn't answer. "Tell me! Or I'll do worse than kill you. I'll rip out your eyes, cut off your tongue, and your fingers. You'll live, but you'll wish you hadn't."

The alchemist made a strangled sound. I loosened the fire rope around his neck. "I-I can't tell you," he croaked.

I stepped closer. "You asked for it."

My fire wrapped around his arm and lifted his hand. Then, a circle of fire appeared around his finger. He screamed as it squeezed and burned, searing through his skin.

"Okay, okay," he rasped. I let go of his finger. "I'll tell you."

I lessened the heat of the fire around him. "Where is it?"

"There." He pointed behind me. "The back of that shelf is fake. There's a storage room inside the wall behind it."

I turned to the tall, wooden bookshelf. After dumping all the books on the floor, I took off the middle shelves, and pried off the back. Like he had told me, there was a small closet in the wall.

I looked around the small space. There were all sorts of things in here—books, boxes, vials, herbs, tools, clothes, and even some pillows. I rummaged through the vials, but the labels weren't clear. "Which one?"

"It's a dark blue liquid in a round vial," he said. "It has a scribbled X on the label."

There was a handful of vials like that. I took one and came back to face him. "Are you sure this is the one?"

"I-I am."

Taking advantage of how my power was stronger when the madness was loose, I reached into the alchemist's mind. He tried to resist me, but he couldn't. I went in and searched for clues about the antidote.

He was telling the truth. This was the antidote.

I left his mind. His head dropped forward, as if a huge weight had lifted from him. Fighting my madness, I extinguished my fire around him. The alchemist fell forward.

I wanted to walk away. I wanted to let him go.

But the madness was too strong. It was too alluring. It took over me too easily. The dark spots around my vision increased; my hands shook harder. My mind tingled with the incoming vision. Fighting against it with all I had, I gritted my teeth and swayed on my feet.

Vial in hand, I started walking backward, intent on leaving the alchemist alive.

At least one among the many I had just killed without mercy.

The madness had another idea.

I stepped out of the house and without any thought, fire appeared at the corners of the cabin. As if it had been doused with gasoline, the fire exploded and spread in the blink of an eye.

The screams of the alchemist rang from inside.

A moment later, the screams died out.

And I ran from the scene.

I DIDN'T MAKE IT FAR.

The fire heart fever had its clutches on me. A vision burst through my mind, and I fell to my knees, wreathing on the ground as the images flashed in my mind.

The fire from the alchemists' cabin spreading through the forest, killing the animals around it. The fire traveled far, reaching the tzigane camp. The people were powerless as the fire consumed the tents and destroyed everything and hurt most of them.

Meanwhile, I stood at a distance, laughing like a wicked witch.

With Damara by my side.

A twinkling started on the back of my mind, then a gentle push. I knew that signature. With a gasp, I opened my mind. Felix and Vira's mind linked with mine.

With their power, they pushed my vision back. Although they couldn't get rid of all of it, I felt like I could breathe again, like I could fight it.

Lifting my head from the ground, I glanced back and saw them as they approached me—the big white lion and the delicate white fox. Felix and Vira were heart animals, as magical as I was, and they had great power.

What are you doing here?

An image of them both beside me filled my head.

You want to help me?

They nodded their furry heads. They let me inside their heads, and I saw that when they learned I had left the camp with Kane, they had come after us. It had taken them a while to find us, but they were here now.

The vision pushed harder, and I gasped as my vision alternated between Felix and Vira and the forest, and the burning camp and Damara.

Slowly, the vision retreated, until finally, it was gone.

I blinked the dark spots away from my vision and looked around. Felix had the back collar of my uniform in his mouth and he dragged me—closer to Kane.

A few more minutes passed and I stopped shaking.

I think I can walk now, I told them in their minds.

Felix didn't let me go for a while longer, until my breathing was back to normal. Then, the lion stopped and looked at me.

"I'm fine," I said, my voice rough, my throat dry. "Thanks to you two."

I reached to them and caressed their heads. They pressed their muzzles against my hands, and I could sense the relief in their minds.

What the hell had happened? I had let the madness take control and killed a bunch of alchemists as if they were worms. I was glad I had gotten the antidote, but I didn't need to kill them all like that.

My stomach turned and I thought I would throw up.

I took a long breath and focused. If I let myself, I would curl up on the ground and cry over the horrible act I committed, but I didn't have time for that. I had to save Kane.

I fished the vial from my pocket—I didn't even remember putting it there—and checked it to make sure it was secured and not missing one drop. Then, I glanced to the animals. "We need to go."

Pushing through my sorrow, through the fatigue settling in my muscles, I ran toward the cave, the heart animals right beside me.

When Felix, Vira, and I made it back to the cave, Kane wasn't moving. Terror turned my insides cold. Pain and fatigue forgotten, I rushed to him. Thankfully, he was sleeping, but his breathing was too shallow and slow for my taste.

"Kane," I called, reaching for his head. "I've brought something for you."

His eyes fluttered open. "Mirella?"

"Yes, it's me."

He blinked. "I can't see you."

My heart squeezed. Was the poison so advanced, he was losing his sight?

"Quickly, drink this." I helped him lift his head. "It's the antidote."

I turned the small vial at his mouth and the liquid dripped past his lips. He grunted and scrunched his nose. "Holy shit."

"Drink it all," I said.

He did, and then he lay back down. I watched him like a mother hen, counting as his ragged breathing didn't improve, and he didn't seem any better.

It's not working, I said to Felix and Vira.

They showed me the image of me glancing at a clock on the wall of my mother's kitchen—they were telling me to give it time.

It wasn't that easy.

But as the minutes ticked away, Kane's breathing became stronger, his color returned to his face, his hands stopped shaking, and finally he opened his eyes and he seemed aware of his surroundings.

I let out a long, relieved breath. Kane was fine; he would be fine. I could cry from joy.

"You did it," he said, sitting up. "I was so damn worried that you set out alone."

"Well, I was alone at first, but then I found some friends." I gestured to Felix and Vira, who were lying at the cave's mouth.

He frowned at them. "How?"

I shrugged. "They told me they wanted to follow us." Kane scooted closer to me. "What are you doing? You should rest more."

He took my hands in his. "I will, I just want to hold you." He tugged me to him, and I sat right beside him, my hip and shoulders pressed against his. "I was scared when you left me here."

I nodded. "I was too."

"Not because of me," he said. "Because you went out alone because of me and I couldn't help you."

I fake-glared at him. "You were afraid because of me? I was terrified because of you. I had just survived an attack, heard an earful about being caught and almost dying, and then what do you do? Almost die. And you didn't even want to tell me about it!" I slapped his shoulder, but then my face fell. "If I had lost you ..." A lump rose to my throat. "By Saint Sara-la-Kali, I don't even want to think about it."

He leaned into me and pressed a soft kiss on my forehead. "Thankfully, we make a good pair and we can help each other."

"True." I pushed his shoulders. "But now you should rest and recover."

Kane didn't resist me. He lay down on the bedroll, but pulled me to him. "Only if you rest with me."

With a smile, I lay beside him. I snuggled against him, my head on his shoulder, while his arms were wrapped tightly around my waist. "Don't you scare me like that ever again."

He snorted. "Look who is talking. You scare me like that all the time."

"Hazards of my job."

"Well, mine is to protect the heart maiden, so me too."

Despite being tired, dirty, having survived a mini-heart attack, hating myself for all the deaths I had caused, and the looming of the mysterious fire flower in our chest, I focused on these glorious minutes, when Kane and I were together and happy with each other again.

That was how I survived being the heart maiden. By living moment by moment before I freaked out and lost it.

Under my head, I felt as Kane's chest slowed down. He was sleeping, and hopefully, he would be able to rest. Clearing my mind of anything else, I concentrated on Kane's breathing and closed my eyes.

9

I was alarmed when Kane and I woke up the next morning. We slept for over eight hours! While we were on a mission. That was unacceptable. Trying to not waste any more time, Kane and I cleaned up at a nearby stream, ate some half-assed breakfast, and packed.

When we were ready to go, Felix and Vira stood in our way.

The animals projected an image of a path between the trees into my mind.

"They want us to follow them," I said.

Kane frowned. "Right now? We should be following the flower's call?"

"I know, but ..." I paused, waiting for the animals to tell me something else. They didn't. "I think it's about the flower.

"I know you trust them." Kane watched them for a moment. "All right, we'll go with you."

The animals led us out of the cave, and back in the forest. After a couple of minutes, I wanted to complain it was taking too long, but at least they didn't veer from the flower's call too much.

Finally, we crossed a line of trees and came upon a big boulder, oddly placed between too tall trees.

Muma Padurii stood on the boulder.

"You two are finally here." She smiled at us. I wasn't sure how I felt about seeing Muma again. With her bark-like skin, long black hair, and flowing white dress, she looked more like a creature from a horror movie than a forest protector. Besides her hideous appearance, all of our encounters had never been easy.

"You were waiting for us?" I asked, wary of why the animals brought Kane and me to her.

"I have so much to tell you," she said, losing the smile.

Kane crossed his arms. "Then make it quick, because we're in a rush."

Muma tsked. "So impatient, warrior. It'll all make sense in a second."

"What are you talking about?" I asked.

She tilted her head and narrowed her eyes at us. "Have you ever wondered about the connection you two share? Why you can't burn him? Or why his power manifests in the same color as yours?"

"Of course we have," I said.

"Do you know about it?" Kane asked.

"Indeed, I do," Muma said. "The heart maiden isn't supposed to be alone. A heart keeper is always born before a heart maiden. He's her protector, her lover, her equal, her other half. The heart keeper's presence keeps the heart maiden from going insane. Without him, she'll go mad."

Kane frowned. "How come we've never heard about this before?"

"Because alongside their heart keepers, the heart maidens were too powerful and uncontrollable," Muma continued. "So many centuries ago, the elder council separated the maidens from the keepers. The existence of a heart keeper has been erased from your history. Usually, a heart keeper is considered a powerful tzigane."

I frowned. "So, Damara's story …"

Muma nodded. "Emilian was Damara's heart keeper. The council killed him with the pretense that he had touched the heart maiden to separate them. That's why Damara went mad." And only grew madder as time passed. "As you can guess, you're Mirella's heart keeper, Kane. You keep her sane and help her access her powers as the heart maiden."

"I see." He was way too serious, making me anxious. "What about the fire flower?"

"The bond between a heart maiden and heart keeper isn't fully sealed until they find the fire flower and absorb its powers together." Muma smiled at us again, clearly amused about her tale. "It's sort of a unification ceremony, actually. Once you perform the ceremony, Mirella will be powerful. Powerful enough to take down mad Damara and save your people."

Kane was quiet for a moment. "So, you're saying Mirella and I are basically soulmates."

Muma nodded. "Precisely."

I held my breath. This was a little too much to take in, but I was more anxious about Kane's reaction. So far, though, he was too solemn about it all.

"And we should find this fire flower and perform the unification ceremony?" Kane asked.

"Yes," Muma said. "The faster you do it, the faster you can go back to your people and defeat Damara."

Kane fell quiet.

I didn't know what to say either.

This was too much to take in. The previous elder council had been hiding the heart keepers from us? And not just from heart maidens, but from everyone. They had lied to us all—again.

I looked at Kane, at the handsome, strong, powerful warrior standing in front of me. My heart and soul and body were already his, and this fact wouldn't change.

Why was it so nerve-wrecking to say all of this out loud?

Because this was big. It was a big change. I knew Kane loved me, but was he ready to be tied down to me like this? Choosing each other was one thing, but being tied by fate? It was another.

Was he ready for this?

"I know this is a lot," I quickly said. "Believe me, I feel the same way." I paused, thinking I should put a shield around my heart. "You don't need to go through with this, you know. We can ignore the call and go home. Or, I can try to take the fire flower by myself. I bet it may work like a normal heart flower, which is always helpful."

He stared at me. "You don't want me to be your heart keeper?"

"That's not what I'm saying." I took a step toward him, but stopped myself before I got too close. "Kane ... I love you and I do believe you're the one for me. But I don't want you to tie yourself to me if that's not what you want. I don't want you to feel pressured, as if you have no other choice but to go through with this. You do have another choice and—"

Kane stepped into me and closed his big hands on my upper arms. "Mirella, stop talking." He leaned into me and brushed his lips against mine. "I love you, Mi, and I can't think of any way better to show you that. I would love to be your heart keeper forever and always."

My heart burst with love and happiness. I wound my arms around his neck and pulled him back to me. I pressed my mouth to his, and he took over the kiss, moving his lips in a sensual rhythm that started a new fire low in my belly.

A low growl-hiss came from Muma. "You two should follow me now."

Kane and I begrudgingly broke apart, but he held my hand.

"Where to now?" I asked.

A small smile took over Muma Padurii's lips. "I'll take you to the fire flower."

***

IT DIDN'T TAKE US LONG TO FIND THE MEADOW I HAD SEEN IN my mind. But even though I had a glance at the fire flower then, nothing prepared me for the real thing.

It was bigger than I imagined, a hand taller than the heart flower. The petals looked smooth, but shone like liquid fire under the sunlight.

"It's exquisite," Kane whispered, his eyes locked on the fire flower.

Like a moth to the flame, I reached for it. A spark of fire snapped from its petals, and I jumped back, a little startled.

"Wait," Muma said. "Choose wisely. Once you pick up the fire flower and perform the unification ceremony, your souls will be intertwined for eternity and there will be no breaking the bond. It is a tie stronger than marriage." She glanced at Kane and me. "Are you sure you really want to do this?"

I hesitated. Why was she asking us that? Was her intention to make me think twice, three times about this?

Kane stepped closer to me and slipped his hand in mine. "I'm sure." He turned his gaze to me, so intense and unwavering. "Mirella, I was lost before I found you. You're my north, the star that guides my path. I'm nothing without you, and I can't imagine my life without you in it. I love you."

"I love you too." A tear rolled down my cheek. "If I had to endure eternity, I would choose you to stay by my side."

He tugged me closer and pressed his lips to mine.

"You two can save that for later," Muma said, waving her hands to separate us.

Smiling, we broke the sweet kiss and turned to the flower.

"Ready?" Kane asked.

"Ready," I said.

Together, Kane and I reached for the fire flower. A spark of fire snapped again, but this time, I didn't pull back. Our hands closed around the long steam and we plucked the flower from the ground. The spark of fire in its petals became a big flame, spreading through the entire flower. Tendrils of fire stretched to our hands, twisting as it enveloped our arms and shoulders, and traveled down our entire bodies. It was a hot fire that didn't burn, a comforting and soothing sensation, strong and pure.

In front of me, Kane swam in a sea of fire. His eyes glowed orange and his skin seemed made of lava. I could only guess I looked the same right now.

But the most amazing thing of all was the tug the flower passed on to us. Something like a thud. A thump. The beat of our hearts syncing. I could feel it, the thump-thump of Kane's heart matching mine, the rush of our blood in the same rhythm, the breath passing in our lungs in the same tempo.

He smiled at me, and I was certain I had never seen a more beautiful person in all my life. And he was my man, my other half, my soulmate. Tears brimmed in my eyes.

The flames grew red and a surge of power traveled from the flower's center to our cores. Its fire fed on my magic, on my fire, making the well bigger, deeper. And this time, I wasn't alone. There was someone else benefiting from this power. I had no idea how the fire flower's power would affect Kane's, but if I could feel mine growing immensely, I could only imagine his could too.

Together, we would be unstoppable.

Suddenly, the flower's color dulled and the magic cut off. But the power it had given us didn't lessen. It stayed inside us, strong and pure and ready.

Oh, so ready.

"It's done," Muma said, her tone bored, as if she hadn't witnessed something miraculous. "You're now one."

Like this was a wedding ceremony, Kane pulled me to him and kissed me. His arms wound around my waist as his mouth moved with mine, soft and gentle and warm. I held on to him, the emotion and love and power overwhelming every nerve in my body.

Finally, after a long while, I pulled back for air. "You're mine now," I whispered, my forehead against his.

"I always was," he whispered back. "I know this will become a common phrase, but I can't help it: I love you, Mirella."

"I love you too." I stood on my tiptoes and brushed my lips to his. Just once, then I pulled back again. "As much as I would like to keep this going, we have company." I jerked my chin to Felix and Vira, who strolled around the flower meadow, as if they hadn't seen anything. Muma Padurii was nowhere to be seen. Had she already left? "We also should go back to camp. Now that we've found the flower and got its power, we have a lot to do."

He nodded. "I know, I know." He let go of me, but held on to my hand. "But just know this. I'm going to want some celebration later."

A shiver ran down my spine. "I can't wait for it."

10

WE HAD BEEN AWAY FOR ALMOST TWO DAYS, AND IT WOULD take us just as long to go back. With the power from the fire flower, our stamina proved to be better than before, and Kane and I were able to run through the forest for a long time, with Felix and Vira leading the way. If we could keep this up, we would be able to cut the traveling time in half.

But we were not vampires or werewolves and had to slow down at times, and even stop for short breaks.

It was almost sunrise when we decided to stop for breakfast. I put down my bag, sat down on the jutting roots of an old tree, and listened to the waking birds and the gentle breeze, and took in a lungful of pine-filled air.

I felt different, and yet, I was still the same. The same hotheaded heart maiden who tried doing the best for everyone, but ended up screwing things up all the time.

But more powerful now.

I looked at my hands, as if I could see the magic flowing inside.

"What is it?" Kane asked as he sat down beside me. He

placed a soft kiss on my shoulder. Despite being in the middle of the forest for a mission, it seemed as though we were newlyweds on our romantic honeymoon.

I took the sandwich from him. "Just wrapping my head around everything. Until a few days ago, we didn't even know there was a fire flower out there. And now you're my heart keeper."

He pressed a hand to his chest. "I'll keep it right here."

I rolled my eyes at him and took a bite of my sandwich. While chewing, I looked down, at my bag and the fire flower peeking from the half closed zipper. I could have folded it, or broken the stem in half to fit it inside, but I wanted to have it whole to show our friends. After all, this was a myth that had come to life.

A few feet from us, Vira and Felix lay in the grass, probably having an entire conversation in their minds. On instinct, I opened up my senses to them. Felix had his mind closed, but Vira was as open as a book.

For some reason, the little female fox was sad.

What happened?

A feeling of surprise hit me hard. It was her, startled by my voice in her head.

She reined in her surprise and showed me the matter: Felix, looking magnificent and strong, with the sun shining on him.

I gasped.

Vira loved Felix.

Why don't you tell him?

An image of him snapping his razor-sharp teeth at her and rejecting her popped in my mind. Vira lay on the ground and whimpered as sadness overcame her.

She was afraid of being rejected by him.

It is a possibility, but how will you ever know if you don't tell him?

She showed me images of herself lost in the middle of a forest during a huge storm.

What was that supposed to mean?

A twig snapping was the only warning we got. The next second, Damara and Trina appeared in front of us.

Several things happened at once. Felix and Vira shot up to attack the duo, but a wall of fire trapped them, Kane pulled his twin swords from his back, and I dropped the last bite of my sandwich and channeled my magic.

"Mirella, Kane," Damara drawled, with a snarky smile. In a dark orange dress and with her long hair floating behind her as if she were underwater, she looked more like an enchanting goddess of fire than a mad heart maiden.

"Trina," Kane rasped. "What's going on?"

Trina shook her head. "You wouldn't understand."

He lowered his swords an inch. "Try me."

But Trina didn't say anything.

It hurt seeing Trina and Damara together. I had wanted to believe that Damara somehow had something over Trina's head, but watching the young woman standing by her side, dressed in warrior garb and holding a sword, ready for a fight, was confirmation that Trina had betrayed us.

I focused on my newfound magic. "What are you doing here?"

"I felt a call, a call I thought was a myth." Damara's gaze dipped to the bag at my feet. "I see it isn't a myth after all. You truly found the fire flower. Give it to me."

"Wait!" Kane took a step forward, his swords turned down. "This is ridiculous. Trina," he said, a hopeful tone to his words. "This isn't you. You wouldn't betray your friends and side with her." He shook his head once. "What's happening? How is she controlling you?"

With my eyes locked on a cackling Damara, I bent down and picked up my bag. She and Trina were here. They had come after hearing the call. Had just Damara heard the call?

Trina's eyes glowed orange. "Give us the fire flower."

I gasped. "You are Damara's heart keeper."

"What?" Kane asked, as shocked as I was.

That was why Trina had betrayed us, because she was connected to Damara, because she loved her.

Damara's smile widened. "Pretty and smart. I knew I always liked you, Mirella. It's a shame we're on the opposite sides of the table." She extended her hand. "Now, give us the flower before I take it by force."

I slung my bag over my shoulders, but instead of putting it on my back, I put it on my chest. The flower was a few inches from my face. "Don't you know what the fire flower does? Kane and I are more powerful now. You can't fight us. You won't win."

Flames covered Damara's hands. "You want to bet?"

She hurled a fire bolt at us. I lifted my hands and took over the flame, sending it sideways. It faded among the trees. Damara didn't relent. She threw bolt after bolt, as if she could hurt me that way.

Meanwhile, Trina came at Kane, her sword raised high.

I turned to help him, but a howl caught my attention. The fire was closing in around Felix and Vira. What the ...? I threw a stream of fire at Damara and worked on the fire around the animals. I channeled its power, forcing it to obey me. I had to send another strike at Damara to keep her busy, until finally, I put the fire out and the animals were free.

They attacked Damara.

She ran from them and came at me.

I flung a powerful spell at her, one with enough magic to stun her if hit in the right spot, or at least make her dizzy, but once more, Damara was too fast. The spell grazed her shoulder—not enough to take her down.

Felix and Vira didn't give up. Big mouths open, they lunged at Damara. This time, she didn't move. Instead, she threw fire bolts at them. Felix fell back, the bolt having hit him in the flank.

But when the bolt hit Vira in the chest, she dropped like a rock. For a moment, I was too stunned to move. Had Damara killed the little fox? Felix let out a terrible roar and jumped Damara.

She saw that coming and dropped him like Vira.

"No," I whispered, shocked.

"Don't worry," Damara said, her voice full of disdain. "They deserve it for trying to kill me, but I didn't hurt them. After all, they are as special as I am. They are stunned for now."

"If you hurt them ..."

"What?" she asked, with a small laughter. "You'll hurt me? I would like to see that."

That was it. This bitch was going down today. My energy renewed by the rage inside me, I ran at her, my hands up, and jets of fire washing over her.

Damara tried creating a fire wall to stop me and sent spells at me, but I was too strong for her. She couldn't win now.

Bracing herself against my magic, Damara lifted her arms and knelt on the ground. She was clearly tired trying to resist me. I sent more power through the fire.

With a gasp, Damara fell to the ground.

My ears pricked with the sound of boots stomping. Too close. Too damn close. I looked up as a dozen or so red alchemists surrounded us.

By Saint Sara-la-Kali ...

I hadn't even noticed that Damara had moved until she threw a bolt of fire at my hands. I flinched and snapped out of my stupor, but by then it was too late. Damara was on top of me and closed her hands around the fire flower.

"No!" I screamed, reaching for it. We both held the flower, tugging as if it was a rope. "Let go, damn it!"

Damara sent a small spark of fire at my feet. "You let it go!"

I tapped around, avoiding her fire and loosening the grip around the fire. "No!" I tugged harder.

And the flower ripped in two.

Damara and I froze, both of us stunned as we looked down at our hands. I had most of the flower's bud and petals, while Damara had a bit of the bud, a couple of petals and most of the stem.

A wicked smiled appeared on her lips. "I win."

Gritting my teeth, I lunged at her.

But she ran the opposite way and a line of alchemists stepped in front of me. Trina was right beside her.

I flung my fire at them. "Get out of my way."

But these red alchemists must have been training with the other heart maiden, because they called their shadow swords and deflected my fire as if it was a fly buzzing around them. I hadn't put all my power in my magic, because I didn't want to hurt them, but that was it. If they didn't want to move their asses out of my way, I would move them.

I created a wave of fire in a half circle and sent it to them. Like a tsunami, it washed over everything in its path. Two alchemists got caught in the wave, but the rest of them ran and regrouped a few yards from me.

Kane stepped to my side. "Are you okay?"

"She got a piece of the fire flower!"

"I saw," Kane said. He bumped his arm on mine. "It's okay. Let's get rid of these alchemists. Then, we go after them and get the flower back."

"Deal."

Kane and I attacked. He swung his swords around, moving like a poisonous snake, and I threw my magic at the alchemists. Although I wanted to kill them, I once more told myself that wasn't me. I wouldn't carelessly kill someone, even if they were my enemies. So, I threw several bolts that numbed upon contact.

Soon, there were several bodies around our feet—either dead by swords, or stunned by fire.

Kane and I looked at each other. It had been at least twenty minutes since Damara and Trina ran away. By now, they were too far away. Moreover, we had no way of telling which direction they had gone.

Damara and Trina were gone.

And they had a piece of the fire flower with them.

11

THE FIRST COUPLE OF HOURS AFTER DAMARA AND TRINA'S attack, we scoured the forest, searching for them. I even called Muma Padurii, knowing that she might have a few things to say to me for hurting her forest, but if she was so deeply connected to the land, she would know where Damara and Trina were.

But Muma didn't come.

Without another choice, I undid the stunning spell on the heart animals, and then they, Kane, and I headed back to our camp.

Dread made my muscles tense as we approached our newest hiding place. We had been away for four days, and even though we had been successful, that victory was short-lived. Now, Kane and I wouldn't be the most powerful couple out there.

After using the fire flower and performing the unification ceremony, Damara and Trina would be our equals, and we would be back at square one.

The mid-afternoon sun was high and hot when we finally

arrived at the camp. Leander and Lash, who had been patrolling the area, saw us approaching and came to greet us.

"You're back," Leander said, genuine contentment on his face.

I glanced at the camp right behind them. It was oddly quiet. "Where's everyone?"

"Some adults have taken the kids down to the stream to cool off," Lash said. "The others are working on their tasks. Cooking, cleaning, gathering fire wood."

"But the council should be in the main tent," Leander said. He extended his hand, inviting us to go there.

Despite the bad news we would have to deliver, I was eager to see my family and friends, to know they were all right while Kane and I were away.

Kane and I headed to the main tent, while Felix and Vira turned toward the stream, probably to cool off too.

"There she is," Ramon said when I stepped into the tent. He and the others were gathered around the table in the center, a big map of the area open over it. "I heard you coming a mile away." Ramon tapped his ear.

"You and your werewolf abilities," I teased.

My mother and Sheila flocked to me, while my father and Ellie smiled at me, their faces shining with relief.

"So, how was it?" Sheila asked, glancing from me to Kane.

"Did you find the flower?" Theron asked, serious.

I pulled the fire flower from inside my bag. A collective gasp bounced through the tent.

"You did it," my mother whispered.

"It wasn't a myth," Cora said.

"It's beautiful," my grandmother exclaimed.

She should have seen it before Damara had plucked some petals and half of the stem from it.

"I have good news and bad news." I braced myself for the onslaught of criticism. "The fire flower is true, as you can see. Kane and I found it and received its power."

"What does it do?" Dolan asked.

Heat spread through my cheeks. "Well, actually, it's a funny story. The fire flower seals a bond between the heart maiden and the heart keeper."

"Heart keeper?" my mother asked. "What's that?"

"It's a tzigane who completes the heart maiden," I explained. "He keeps her from going insane, and after the bonding ceremony with the fire flower, the heart keeper makes the heart maiden more powerful."

Theron stared at Kane. "That means ..."

"I'm Mirella's heart keeper," Kane announced.

In the back of the room, Artan unfolded from a low chair and narrowed his eyes at us. "Heart keeper. That's bullshit. There's no such thing."

By Saint Sara-la-Kali, I had hoped he wouldn't be here.

Kane stood tall and his voice was proud beside me. He had never let anyone intimidate him, much less Artan. "Basically, I'm her soulmate," Kane said, daring Artan to defy him. If they went for another fist fight, I would kick both their asses.

"Let me get this straight," Theron started. "You mean that two hundred years ago, Emilian was Damara's heart keeper? That's why the elder council killed him?"

I nodded. "Right. They wanted to keep the heart keeper away from the heart maiden so they could control her. They created that stupid rule that the heart maiden couldn't be touched."

"That's absurd," Artan muttered.

I ignored him and went on. "However, fate decided to be funny and gave Damara a second heart keeper."

"What?" Ramon asked. "Is that possible?"

I shrugged. "It seems to be, because Trina is Damara's new heart keeper."

Silence fell through the tent. Everyone was stunned with the news.

"That's why she betrayed us," Ellie said. Her face fell. "That's why she tried to poison you." And killed Kizzy instead.

I nodded.

"That's okay," Sheila said. "You two have the fire flower." She pointed to the flower in my hands. "And they don't."

I looked down to the ground. "They attacked us on our way back and got a piece of the flower."

"What?" Artan shrieked. He pointed to Kane and me. "You two don't deserve all this power and responsibility. You—"

"Artan, shut up!" Theron stepped in his way. "Leander, Lash, take him out. And if he fights you, you're allowed to knock him out."

"Hey!" Artan protested as Leander and Lash hooked their arms around his shoulders and dragged him out. "Take your hands off me!"

We remained frozen until his yells stopped, either because he had given up, or because Leander and Lash had to put him out.

With a sigh, Theron returned to the table in the center. "Have you two performed the ceremony yet?"

My cheeks warmed again. "Yes."

"And you think Damara and Trina will be able to do the same with the flower piece they stole?" he asked.

Kane nodded. "Yes."

"We need to kill them both right now, before they use the fire flower," Ramon suggested. "I'll gather my wolves."

"We don't know where they are," my father said. "First, we need to locate them. Second, we need a plan."

"I seriously hate Trina," Ellie whispered.

"Honestly, I'm not sure Trina is that bad," I said. Everyone in the room looked at me as if I had lost another screw. "I'm serious. I think she lost her way, and ended up finding it with the wrong person. I don't think she's bad. Her actions might have been rash—no, terrible, actually—but I think she's confused."

"What are you suggesting?" Theron asked. "That we don't kill Trina?"

"Next, you're going to tell us to not kill Damara too," Ramon added.

I didn't say anything, because honestly, if I could, I wouldn't kill anyone. I would rather take out their powers and put them in a special prison, where they were comfortable, but contained. We had done that with the elder council, and it had worked, until the enclave had been invaded.

By Damara.

"I don't know," I muttered, feeling lost myself.

My grandmother stared at me. "As the elder of this group, I have a request all of you can't deny."

"What is it?" my father asked.

"I would like us to forget about Damara, the alchemists, and the war for the rest of today," she said. "Just tonight. No talk about fights and strategies and our enemies." A soft smile spread over her lips. "Instead, I would like celebrate the special bond between my *puri chey* and her heart keeper."

My mother gasped. "You're right. Mirella and Kane are

practically married now. Soulmates, how romantic!" She rushed to me and gathered my hands in hers. "My only child has found her match and we should celebrate it."

My father put an arm around Kane's shoulders, startling the big warrior. "That's right. Marriages are a big deal for tziganes, and apparently, this bond you two share is even more special. We need to celebrate."

"But what about—?"

Sheila shot a glare at Theron, shutting him up. "This is an old woman's request and you will obey it."

"*Puri daj*," I started, my tone low. "I think Theron is right. We're wasting time and—"

"No, I won't have it." Sheila shook her head vehemently. "Like Dolan said before, we don't know where Damara and Trina are right now. By all accounts, they could have already performed the bond. We won't stop them in time. And it would be good to have one little respite, one special celebration to bring smiles to our people's faces, before we search for Damara."

We were all quiet for a moment, thinking about what my grandmother said. She was right. We needed to gather our warriors and Ramon's wolves, and it would be dark soon. We had no idea where to go as well. Stopping Damara and Trina from performing the bonding ceremony wasn't an option. Now, we had to prepare for the aftermath.

But before that, we could give our people one more night of festivities, good food, and a good time, before we faced the biggest fight of our lives.

"What do you think?" I asked Kane.

With a smile, he reached over and entwined his fingers around mine. "I would love to celebrate our bond."

My mother practically melted at his feet, my father

slapped Kane's shoulders hard, and my grandmother clapped her hands once loudly. "That's it, people. Let's get a party ready in record time," she said.

"All right," Ramon said with a sigh. "As the brother of the bride, I have to take care of the groom." He beckoned ~~to~~ Kane to follow him.

"What?" I squealed. "Bride? Groom? We aren't getting married, Ramon. We don't need to. We just want to celebrate our union, the one that already happened."

"Whatever." Ramon waved his hand at me, dismissing me.

Theron shook his head, but helped Ramon and Dolan, and the four of them disappeared from the tent.

"And you're with us," Ellie said with a huge smile. She was definitely more excited about this than I was.

But how could I resist them? When my mother, my grandmother, Ellie, and Cora guided me out of the main tent, I let them. I rolled my shoulders, took a deep breath, and tried relaxing while they pampered me.

The night would probably be fun, but the preparation would be torture.

12

───────

GETTING READY WASN'T AS BAD AS I THOUGHT IT WOULD. Knowing they would have liked to participate, Ellie had called Ryane, and Cora had called Violet. The six women and I occupied my mother's tent while we got ready. I had no idea where they had gotten so many colorful dresses and jewelry —if I remembered correctly, we had fled the enclave and barely grabbed anything in the process—but suddenly a sea of green and blue and pink and orange fabrics inundated the tent.

I behaved like a doll, standing there, while they did my hair, applied my makeup, and dressed me up.

But after they were done, I stood in front of a cheap standing mirror and smiled at my reflection.

My hair was tied up in a thick French braid until my neck, then the braid opened up, letting my curls fall down to the middle of my back. My makeup was simple, but pretty, with smoky eyes and red lipstick.

Then, there was my outfit. The top had a squared cleavage and short sleeves, and many tiny crystals all over it.

The skirt started low on my hips, leaving my entire midriff exposed, hugging my bosom, but opening up in a great quantity of fabric at my feet. A slit showed my left leg when I walked. But the most beautiful thing was the fabric. The deep red color shone orange and dark pink when I moved.

"Exquisite," my mother whispered from behind me. Her eyes met mine in the mirror. "I'm so proud of you."

I shook my head. "I don't see why."

She grabbed my shoulders and turned me to her. "Mirella, how can you say that? You've saved us so many times."

"But I lost so many people too," I said quickly. "A lot of people have suffered because of me."

"That's what happens in a war, sweet Mi," she whispered. "We may have lost a lot of friends, but we would have lost many more if you hadn't intervened." She rested a hand on my chest, just above my heart. "Despite your stubbornness, you have a good heart, a pure heart, and I'm sure if you follow it, it'll never lead you astray."

I smiled at her. "Thanks, Mom."

She pulled me into a tight hug. I rested my head on her shoulder, enjoying the moment.

My mother and I never had an easy relationship. Since I was little, she had lied to me about our origins. Because of her lies, I had hated her. I had thought she was crazy. I had purposely been mean to her, and left her behind. But we had found out way—with a few bumps in the road. Now, our relationship was stronger than I would have thought it could be, and I knew it would only get stronger from here.

"Time to go," Sheila announced.

My mother and I broke the embrace, but we kept our hands linked as we walked out of the tent.

In less than two hours, we had organized the party, and the camp had been transformed. Colorful lamps flanked the streets formed by the tents. We followed one of the paths to the edge of the camp, where the lamps opened up, forming a wide circle. Long, rectangular tables and wooden chairs rested between the lamps, adorned with big flower arrangements and many plates of food and bottles of various drinks. The air was heavy with cinnamon, paprika, and grape scents.

The tziganes, all dressed in the finest clothes they owned, and a handful of wolves from Ramon's pack stood behind the tables, waiting. I saw the familiar faces of Leander, Lash, Cora, Rye, Neil, Ryane, Tomas, Jayme, Bryna, and their baby, Marie, Anne, Violet, and more.

Right in the center of the circle formed by the lamps, Kane stood, with my father and my two half-brothers behind him. Under the stars and the glow of the colorful lights, Kane's skin looked tanner than usual. His longish hair was pulled back, showing off all the sharp edges of his handsome face. Surprisingly, he wasn't wearing black. Instead, he had downed a fancy, formal white shirt, a red sash made of the same fabric as my outfit, and dark gray pants.

He looked breathtakingly gorgeous, and he was all mine.

As if this was a real wedding, my father walked to the edge of the lamp circle and extended his hand to me. My mother urged me forward. I took my father's hand and let him guide me back to the center.

Kane smiled at me, radiant and strong. Not even a little bit nervous—if he was, he didn't let it show. After bowing his head to my father, Kane took both my hands and turned to me. Hands entwined, we stood together in the middle of the circle.

"We're here to celebrate the special, magical union of

Mirella and Kane—heart maiden and heart keeper," my father said, loud and proud. While we got ready for the party, the news of the fire flower and our bond spread like wildfire, and by now everyone in the camp had heard what happened —or some version of it. Thankfully, we were able to keep the information that Damara had stolen a piece of the flower to ourselves. "We wish Saint Sara-la-Kali to bless you both now and forever. That you lead a fair and prosperous life, helping and caring for your fellow tziganes, and for yourselves." My father raised his arms. "Let's celebrate!"

The tziganes cheered and music started—a trio played instruments at one side of the circle. My family and friends crowded around Kane and me, congratulating us and wishing us the best. Around us, the tziganes started dancing, chatting, eating, and drinking.

It was a real party, which made me content. It was great to see the tziganes having a good time for once. The last party we hosted had been a real wedding, and that had ended tragically. This time, I prayed for Saint Sara-la-Kali to keep any bad happenings and news away from us until at least tomorrow morning.

Kane spun me under his arm, then pulled me against him, dancing in rhythm to the fun flamenco song playing.

He leaned on me and asked, a whisper in my ear, "Are you happy?"

I wrapped my arms around his shoulders. "Very."

"Me too." He pressed a soft kiss on my neck, and a shiver rolled down my spine. His arms tightened around my waist, his hands splayed on the bare skin of my back, pressing me against him. "I love you so fucking much."

I inhaled his strong, spicy scent. "I love you too."

His lips trailed up my jaw, across my cheek, and—

"May we cut in?" my father asked.

Mortified, I sprang apart from Kane. "Sure."

My mother was right next to Dolan. While my father took me for a dance, Kane spun around with my mother.

My father smiled at me, his greenish eyes warm. "You seem happy."

I nodded. "I am."

"Kane seems happy too."

I stole a glance at Kane and my mother. He laughed at something my mother said. By Saint Sara-la-Kali, I hoped she wasn't telling him about how stubborn and plain annoying I was when I was a child.

"I think so too," I said with a smile.

"I'm proud of you, Mirella."

I returned my gaze to my father. What was it with him and my mother saying this today? Well, at least knowing they thought so highly of me warmed my heart. "Thank you."

"I wish ... I wish I had known about you earlier," he said, his voice thick. "I wish I could have been there for all of your milestones and important occasions. Unfortunately, I can't change the past. But I can guarantee that I'll be here, no matter what, in the future."

My eyes misted. I wouldn't cry right now, I wouldn't cry right now!

I sniffed, trying to contain the tears. "*Nais tuke, daj.*"

His eyes widened. It was probably the first time I called him *daj*. But it wouldn't be the last.

Before we could talk more, Theron stepped in and danced with me.

"Earlier, I sent out a few warriors to search for Damara and Trina," he announced, all serious.

I narrowed my eyes at him. "As much as I appreciate how

much you care and want to solve everything, I thought tonight was a night for celebration."

"It is, but that doesn't mean we can let our guard down." He glanced out, past the circle formed by the colorful lamps. I was sure he was trying to spy the warriors patrolling the camp's perimeter. "We might take a breather, but the war isn't over."

"Theron, can you try to relax for a few minutes?" I genuinely wanted him to have a good time. He used to be so much fun, but since things—everything—took a turn for the worst, he had been all business, all the time.

"I'll make sure he does," Ellie said. With a smile, she extended her hand to him.

"Yes, please, take your boyfriend and show him a good time." I winked and placed Theron's hand in hers.

She winked at me and took Theron for a spin.

For a moment, I stood in the middle of the fray, with everyone dancing around me, laughing and smiling and chatting. By Saint Sara-la-Kali, it was so great seeing everyone like this.

Until Artan weaved through the crowd and walked toward me.

His hair was disheveled, his sash was loose around his waist, and his shirt was buttoned wrong—but at least he had buttoned it this time. Eyes on me, he took a sip of his silver flask, then stashed it in the waist of his pants at his back.

Halting right in front of me, he bent at the waist in an exaggerated bow. "May I have this dance?"

I hesitated, wishing I could say no. I mean, I could, but it felt wrong to deny him this much on this day. Besides his self-destruction, we had shared good moments before, and I wished I could look back with fondness in my heart, not hate, not disgust.

"Sure," I said.

He wound an arm around my waist, pulling me close to him, and took my right hand in his left. His alcohol stench washed over me, and I almost pulled away. Why was he drinking so much lately? He would kill himself this way.

"You know, even before, when I was your warrior and Kizzy was only my fiancée, I thought we would find a way of making it work, of being together." His voice was low, sorrowful. "I thought we would have a ceremony like this." His eyes rose above my head, and I was sure he was staring daggers at Kane somewhere. "I was supposed to be your heart keeper, not that stranger."

Why, oh why was he saying this to me now? "Artan ..."

"Just hear me out."

"No, Artan, you hear me out." I slowed down, wanting to make sure he was paying attention to what I was going to say and nothing else. "I'm sorry ... for everything. I'm sorry it didn't work out between us, I'm sorry about Kizzy, I'm sorry about Kane. And I'm definitely sorry to see what you're doing to yourself right now. Please, Artan ... you used to be such an amazing warrior, strong and full of honor. I know a lot has happened, and it all hurts, but please, try to pull yourself together. Try to stop drinking, to start helping, to be yourself again." I paused. "And more importantly, please, please, let me go."

He stared at me, his drunk eyes having a hard time focusing. "It's hard," he confessed, his voice a low whisper lost among the music and chatter.

"I know. I know it is." I patted his shoulder. "But I believe in you. I always have. If anyone can heal from this, it's you."

As if he was coming to the realization of what he was doing, Artan's brows curled down and he stopped dancing. Slowly, he lowered his arms and stepped back. "I'm sorry," he muttered before whirling on his heels and marching away.

Once more, I stood in the middle of the crowd, with a heavy ball inside my chest. I thought about going after him, but that wouldn't be right. I couldn't keep going after him when I was asking him to let me go. I had to believe, like I said I did, that he could save himself. That he wanted to do it. Meanwhile, I had to live my life. Tonight, I focused on the happiness overflowing around me, on my beautiful family and friends, and on the man I loved.

The rest ... I would worry about the rest tomorrow.

"Looking for me," Kane whispered in my ear.

I turned around and found him right there, standing behind me. "I was."

He opened his arms. "I'm here, and I think I already danced with all the women in the enclave, so I'm all yours now."

I chuckled. "You better be."

I stepped to him and he embraced me. I rested my cheek on his chest, where I could hear his strong heart, beating in synchrony with mine. He dipped his head, his chin on the top my head. Like that, we danced, a slow song that was only playing through our bodies, being carried by the blood in our veins.

We swayed side to side for a little while, enjoying each other's company, and watching as our family and friends danced. My mother danced with my father, Neil with Sheila, Theron had Ellie, Ramon spun around with Violet, and Ryane was with Tomas. Even Cora had stopped arguing with

Rye for once, and she had conceded way too many dances to him.

If only I could stop time. If only we could be this happy and united all the time. One day, we would be. One day soon, I hoped. After we defeated Damara and her army, we would be free and plain happy.

A tiny pang cut through my chest.

We would defeat Damara, and that meant killing Trina too. Despite all that she had done, Trina had helped us so many times. I would never forget when she defied the elder council with me and brewed a potion using alchemy. Because of that, we had been able to save many tziganes from succumbing to the soulless spell.

How could a person like that be evil?

Then, I remembered she tried poisoning me, and killed Kizzy instead.

And I wasn't so sure anymore.

"What's going through that pretty head of yours?" Kane asked, his voice soft.

"Nothing," I said. "Everything."

"What do you mean?"

"It's so good to see everyone having a great time. It's starting to dawn on me that in a couple of hours the party will end, and we'll get ready for another battle."

"That's life," Kane said with a sigh. "Full of ups and downs. What we need to do is enjoy the ups, and fight through the downs with all we have."

I pulled back and looked at him. "What are you? A motivational speaker?"

He chuckled. "As if. I'm more likely to bring out my swords and slash first, speak later."

I shook my head. "Look at that, you're funny too."

"Funny, hmm." He dipped into me and brushed his lips on mine. "No, not funny. I can be *fun*, though." He dragged his mouth to my ear and whispered, "Want to get out of here so I can show you how much fun I can be?"

A wave of heat rolled through me, curling my toes and tightening my belly. Breathless, I nodded.

With my hand secured in his, Kane led us out of the lamp circle, through the streets among the tents, to his tent at the edge of the camp. We had all been assigned tents with multiple people in it—mine was with Cora, Ryane, Ellie, and me—but Kane had snatched a small one and claimed it was only his from the beginning.

Now, I was grateful for that.

Kane pushed me inside the tent, which barely came up to my shoulders, and immediately fell over me. He had his arm around my waist and softened my fall, though I wouldn't have been hurt with the thin mattress underneath.

He pushed to his knees and closed the zipper of the tent's flap, then he stayed there, watching me through the darkness.

I waved my hand and a small flame appeared in my open palm. "Better this way."

"Much." His intense eyes devoured every inch of me.

I turned the flame into a small dim orb and sent it floating on the top of the tent. Batting my lashes and biting my lower lip, I jutted my index finger out and beckoned Kane to come to me.

Pushing my skirt aside, his hands smoothed up my legs. He shook his head.

I dropped my hands. "Then at least take off your shirt so I can drool too."

He raised an eyebrow at me. "Only if you take off yours too."

For half a second, I hesitated, too self-conscious. But when I remembered that he loved me, that he liked my body, I emboldened. I reached for the hem of my blouse right below my ribs and pulled it over my head. Naked from the waist up—I hadn't been wearing a bra since the blouse had built-in support—I lay down and beckoned him to do the same.

Oh, so ever slowly, he unbuttoned his shirt, button by agonizing button, while his eyes shone with pure hunger. His gaze was like a caress. I could feel it in my skin, driving me crazy.

Finally, Kane threw his shirt off, but he didn't waste much time appreciating the view. Instead, he dipped into me and took one of my breasts in his mouth. I cried out and arched my back as he sucked hard and bit my nipple.

He dragged his mouth lower, around my bellybutton. "Tell me what you want," he urged, his voice husky.

Desire and heat flared through every nerve of my body. "You, oh, I want you."

Kane bunched up my skirt around my hips. Thinking he wanted to take it off, I raised my hips. "Nu-uh." He held the skirt and crawled lower.

And lower.

Until he disappeared under the skirt.

By Saint Sara-la-Kali …

I clamped a hand over my mouth before I screamed in desire, but I couldn't control my rapid breathing as Kane pleasured me, making me see stars, and feel the fire inside my veins.

When I climaxed, my skin turned orange.

With a smile, Kane crawled over me. "I like you like this.

It means you're losing control. I love it when you lose control."

He pressed his body to mine, and once more, I was amazed that I couldn't burn him—but now we knew why. I wrapped my arms and legs around him, caging him in and planning on never letting him go.

"Make me lose control again," I whispered.

He groaned. "My pleasure."

His mouth crashed against mine, and he kissed me as if he was dying. As if I was an oasis in the desert. As if I was the heart maiden to his heart keeper.

Without breaking the earth-shaking kiss, Kane grabbed my bunched up skirt and tugged me to him. He slipped inside me, and I gasped in pure pleasure—when had he taken off his pants?

He used the skirt to pull me to him, to thrust into me harder, deeper. But soon his skin was as orange as mine, and the faint smell of smoke spread through the tent. The skirt and the white sheets were burning.

"Shit," I muttered. Inhaling deeply, I channeled the fire, calling it back. The fire retreated, leaving behind a half black skirt and bedsheets.

"We don't need this anymore." Kane ripped off the skirt before starting to move again, tearing little moans from my throat.

Being with Kane, making love to him, feeling this complete and satisfied, and yet needing more and more and more ... it was paradise. My heart could burst with all the feelings inside me and the sensations under my skin.

Kane and I continued our rough and loving night for as long as we could endure it—our sweat-covered bodies rubbing together, our breaths mingled, our heartbeats in sync.

The last thing I remembered was snuggling in his arms, after making blissful love, and looking at his handsome face, wishing I could dream of him.

13

THE NEXT MORNING, I DIDN'T WANT TO GET OUT OF BED. Could anyone blame me? The bedsheets were burned, but the mattress was still soft enough, and the naked man beside me had his strong arms around me. His scent was too alluring, and the memories we made last night still too fresh.

In here, everything was perfect and still. Quiet. Peaceful.

Once we got dressed and stepped out, the real world would come crashing down on us. I would have to don my heart maiden mantle and help make decisions that certainly would involve the death of too many people.

Kane rubbed his nose on my cheek. "We do have to get up at some point. You know that, right?"

I groaned and buried my face in his chest. "Five more minutes."

He chuckled. "I bet that if we don't get up in five minutes, someone will come after us. Do you want them to see us like this?" He gestured at our intertwined and naked bodies.

He had a point but ... "We burned my skirt. I have no clothes to put on."

"Fuck." Gently, he disentangled himself from me and sat up. "I'll go get your clothes."

I wrapped my arms and legs around him and tried to pull him down again. "No, not yet."

He grabbed one of my legs and planted a kiss on the top of my foot. "Quit being so stubborn."

I grinned. "I can't help it."

"Don't I know it?" He winked at me.

Despite my protests, Kane put on his black clothes—shirt, pants, and vest—and his black boots, placed a soft peck on my shoulder, then left the tent.

I groaned, a little disappointed he had really left me there. But I knew I was overreacting.

With a sigh, I sat up, holding the still intact blanket over my body. It was time. We had relaxed, had fun, made love, made promises ... now it was time to gear up and plan a war.

Kane came back with my warrior's uniform and boots, and I got dressed under his fierce gaze. When I was done, I got up, a little hunched so I could stand, and twirled in place.

"Not as glamorous as last night's outfit, hm?" I liked the fitted pants, thermal shirt, and vest, but it was nothing like the skirt and blouse I had on last night.

Kane crawled to me. "No, but a lot more badass." He tugged me down, making me fall on my knees on the mattress. His eyes shining orange, he cupped the nape of my neck, and pulled me to him. His mouth met mine, and he kissed me with love and fervor.

"If you keep that up," I whispered against his mouth, "we won't leave this tent before tomorrow."

The corner of his lips tugged up. "That wouldn't be so bad." He deepened the kiss, taking my breath away. Then, he pulled away. "But we really should get going." After a long exhale, the orange glow of his eyes was gone.

This was it. The loving, happy break was gone.

Holding my hand, Kane guided me out of the tent. The sun was starting to rise above the trees over the camp, and most tziganes were still asleep—except for the council members and the warriors.

My mother, my father, my grandmother, Theron, and Ellie were already in the main tent when Kane and I arrived. Everyone seemed tired, as if they hadn't slept all night either. Ellie shot me an I-know-what-you-did-last-night look and my cheeks warmed.

I approached Theron around the table with the map. "Have your scouts come back?"

"They have," he said, his tone severe.

"And?"

The rest of the council arrived with a few warriors—Ramon, Artan, Cora, Rye, Ryane, Tomas, Leander, and Lash. Cora and Rye carried baskets with bagels and coffee, and they passed it around as we settled around the table for our meeting.

I grabbed a bagel and a cup of coffee, suddenly anxious. The tension in the tent was palpable.

Artan stood right across the table from me, looking sober for once. A moment later, I felt Kane's hand on my back, as if to assure himself that I was still there and wasn't going anywhere. I wished I could make all his insecurities disappear.

Theron cleared his throat. "All right, now that we're all here, we'll start. As some of you know, I sent a few scouts out last night to search for Damara and Trina. Unfortunately, they didn't find them. From what the scouts told me, the duo isn't at Lovell, though the place is still crawling with revenants and red alchemists."

"So, what do we do now?" Ramon asked.

"Well, the scouts didn't find Damara and Trina, but they found something else," Theron said. "Not far from here, they found an abandoned mine." He pointed to the mine on the map. Its position formed a triangle with the Lovell enclave and our current camp. "It has been occupied by red alchemists, and it seems they are performing some kind of ritual."

"Ritual?" Dolan asked.

"Yes, but they aren't sure what," Theron continued.

"Does that matter?" Artan asked. Though he seemed sober, he also seemed to be in a terrible mood. "We're after Damara and Trina at the moment, not alchemists."

"I plan on sending more scouts out to search for them, but meanwhile, we shouldn't sit still and wait," Theron said. "I say we take a small group and go check out whatever these alchemists are doing at the mine."

Artan scoffed.

"I think that's a good idea," Rye said.

"Me too," Kane said.

I glanced at Kane. "We'll go." He nodded at me.

"Not only the two of you," my mother protested.

"I'll go too," Theron said.

"And me," Ramon said.

Ellie and Ryane offered to go too, but Theron protested that if it was dangerous, he would rather Ellie stay behind. Artan and Tomas said the same thing to Ryane.

Sheila insisted we take a larger group, but we assured her it was just a surveillance mission. We wouldn't engage unless we had to. Once we discovered what they were doing, we would plan accordingly.

In the end, only Theron, Ramon, Kane, and I geared up to go. After many warnings and well wishes from our parents and grandmother, my brothers, my heart keeper, and I set out toward the abandoned mine.

On the way, Theron and Ramon played the big brothers' role, trying to intimidate Kane. They said things like "if you break her heart, I'll break your face." It was embarrassing, honestly. Thankfully, Kane kept walking proud and confident by my side, not one bit affected by the teasing.

Like the scouts said, the mine wasn't too far and it was abandoned. The lift that once took people down to the mine was gone and only its mechanisms remained, rusty and broken.

Hiding in the shadows of the trees, Theron pointed to the building beside the elevator. "The scouts said they are inside." The wooden building had busted windows, fallen boards, and a broken roof.

It looked like a haunted house.

Kane glanced around. "I don't see any patrols."

"The scouts said they didn't either," Theron said. "Apparently, whatever they are doing inside is keeping them busy."

Ramon pointed to a trellis going up the side of the building, a few feet from a balcony. "We can go up through there."

I narrowed my eyes, because honestly, neither the trellis nor the balcony seemed like they would support our weight, but before I could protest, the guys hurried to the side of the building.

I followed them.

Despite the dead vines swirling around the rotten wood,

the trellis was stronger than it looked. It didn't even creak as we climbed up and landed on the balcony.

We crept toward the doors with broken glass and spied inside. We waited a few minutes, but didn't see any alchemists on the second floor. Slowly, Ramon pushed open the door and we stepped inside.

The place seemed dark, but we could hear a low chatter coming from below. Then, our eyes adjusted and we saw that the building was one large, tall room, and we were on some kind of narrow walkway that wrapped around the entire place.

The guys and I crawled on the dusty wooden floor to the edge of the walkway and peered over the edge.

The floor below was clear of furniture and machinery, which had been pushed to the edges of the room. A large dark red circle had been painted on the floor—was that blood?—and small bowls with a dark liquid were spread every few feet on the perimeter of the circle.

An alchemist dragged the body of a revenant from the center of the circle, dark blood smearing the floor and smudging the drawn lines.

A chill rolled down my spine.

"Fuck this," one alchemist said. He was the only one not wearing their usual masks. "We have to start over. Clean this up!"

A few alchemists stepped into the circle and cleaned the blood. Then, with their shadow swords, they cut their palms and dripped blood over the lines, making them thicker.

"What the hell are they doing?" Theron whispered.

A question that I didn't have an answer for yet.

"All right, I think we're good," the unmasked alchemist said once the circle was cleaned and redone. "Take your positions." Several alchemists and revenants—the scouts hadn't mentioned those—stood around the border of the circle. "This Anasztaz shit …" the unmasked muttered.

"The anas what?" Theron asked in a low voice.

I shrugged.

Below, the unmasked alchemist stood in the center in the circle, a bowl of dark liquid in his hands. He chanted in a strange language. The others joined in. As if in a trance, the unmasked alchemist swayed to one side, then the other. He spilled a little of the dark liquid on the floor, then set the bowl down. Still chanting, he retreated from the circle, taking a place among the others. The alchemists and the revenants dipped their fingers in the bowls and sprayed a few drops of the dark liquid inside the circle.

Then, the dark red lines started bubbling, the entire building shook, and the alchemists tensed.

"Hold it!" the unmasked alchemist said. He raised his voice, his chanting getting louder and louder.

Black smoke rose from the blood lines.

An invisible explosion shook the building. A few windows broke, a couple of tiles on the roof fell, and about half of the revenants and the alchemists dropped to the floor like stones.

Blood pooled around them.

"What the fuck?" Kane whispered.

"Shit," the unmasked said. "It didn't work. Again!" He kicked the body of a revenant beside him. "Clean this fuck up and start over. Now!"

I stared in horror. Whatever they were doing had killed half of them, and they were going to do it again? What was wrong with them?

Theron tugged at my arm. "Let's go."

Glad to get out of there, I nodded.

WE WERE MOSTLY QUIET ON THE WAY BACK TO THE CAMP. WE had tried making sense of what we had seen, but couldn't. I had half a mind to stay behind and find out what the hell the alchemists were up to, but the second half of my mind was dominated by fear. If we stayed there, who said we wouldn't be affected by their spell and drop like flies too? Also, the longer we stayed there, there was a bigger chance we would be found, and we were only four against some crazy red alchemists and a few revenants.

So we went back to the camp. Hopefully, someone would have some insight in what we just witnessed.

The sun was already starting its descent when we arrived back at the camp. The council wasn't in the main tent, so we agreed to go looking for them and meet back there in fifteen minutes. Kane went with me, and our first stop was the kitchen tent, because we were starving. Thankfully, my mother, Sheila, and Ellie were there too.

"Meet us in the main tent in a few minutes," I told them while I put together a quick sandwich for me. Beside me, Kane grabbed an apple and bit into it.

Next, we stopped by the infirmary tent, where we found Ryane and Tomas. I passed on the same message to them, then headed back to the main tent with Kane.

Theron and Ramon were already there with Dolan. Soon, the rest of the group arrived, and for the second time that day, we gathered around the table.

"First things first," Theron started. "Have the scouts come back?"

Dolan shook his head. "Not yet."

"I thought so," Theron muttered.

Across the table, Artan crossed his arms. "So, was it worth it to go check out the alchemists?"

He might be sober today, but his mood was worsening throughout the day. I didn't want to hate him, but I seriously wished he would stop coming to these meetings, at least for now.

"To be honest, we don't know what we saw," Ramon said, his tone flat. Like Theron, Kane, and I, he was too shocked by what we witnessed.

"What do you mean?" my mother asked, worried.

Kane explained what we saw—the circle drawn in blood, the bowls with dark liquid, probably a potion of some kind, the red alchemists and the revenants, their position and their chanting. And then, the sudden death of half of them.

Ellie's face paled. Ryane gasped.

"What were they chanting?" my father asked.

I shook my head. "I don't know. We couldn't understand it, but they did mention a strange word before the chanting. What was it?" I racked my brain, trying to remember it.

"Asas something," Theron said.

I frowned. "No, it was anas something."

"Anasztaz," my grandmother said, her tone somber, her face as pale as Ellie's.

"Yes!" I snapped my fingers. "That's it. What is it?"

"Nothing good." A long sigh passed her lips. "Anasztaz is an ancient titan that devours magical beings. He conjures fiends who do his bidding and go after his victims."

"A titan?" Ellie asked, her eyes wide. "You mean, like in Greek mythology?"

"All legends have a bit of truth," Sheila said in way of an answer.

"I've heard of that myth before," my father said.

"Of course you did," Sheila said. "I always liked myths and legends, and I made sure to teach you and Neil about all of the ones I knew when you two were kids."

"Wait, back up." Theron raised a hand. "*Puri daj,* you're saying the alchemists are trying to summon a titan? What for? To come after us?"

"That's the only reason I see why they would do it," Sheila said.

"But you said they devour all magical beings," I said. "Aren't the alchemists some kind of magical being too? And the revenants? Won't this Anasztaz turn against them?"

"I don't know," Sheila said with a shrug.

"The alchemists must believe they have a way of controlling him," Dolan mused. "Maybe through some kind of potion or spell. Otherwise, they wouldn't try to summon him."

Sheila shook her head, her white braid barely moving. "They can't control the titan. If the myths are correct, nobody can control Anasztaz. Once they summon the titan, it'll devour every magical being in its path."

"What happens when all the magical beings are gone?" Ramon asked. "After it devours the alchemists, the revenants, the tziganes, the werewolves, what will this Anasztaz do?"

"I can't be sure, as this legend is very old," Sheila said. "But I imagine it would start devouring anyone and everyone."

"You mean humans," Ellie whispered.

"Which means, this titan doesn't pose a danger only to us,

but to everyone," I said. The claws of dread inside my chest were cold and strong.

My grandmother. "Correct."

"You say Anasztaz can't be controlled, but there must be a way of stopping him, right?" Artan asked a hint of worry in his voice.

"I don't know," Sheila answered. "The legend I know doesn't mention anything like that."

"We need to stop it," Kane said, his tone resolute. "We need to stop the alchemists and revenants before they summon this titan."

"You're right," I said. "If they are successful in summoning the titan, we'll have bigger problems to worry about than Damara and Trina."

"Agreed," Theron said.

Mutters of "yes," "I agree," and "let's do this" filled the tent.

"You want to go now?" my mother asked. "It's going to be dark soon."

"It doesn't matter," I said. "We need to go as fast as we can. It'll be worse if we wait until morning, then we're attacked in the middle of the night by an unstoppable titan."

My mother flinched, and Ellie pressed a hand to her belly, clearly feeling sick.

"All right, let's put a team together," Theron said, his boss-voice on. "We leave in thirty minutes."

14

COULD THIS DAY BE ANY LONGER? WE HAD AWAKEN AT SUNRISE, went on a mission, had two tense council meetings, and now, as the sun was setting, we were leaving for another mission.

This time though, the group was much larger. Besides Kane, Theron, Ramon, and I, a bunch of tziganes had joined us—Dolan, Artan, Cora, Rye, Tomas, Leander, Lash, Rick, and two other warriors named Samuel and Pablo.

Fourteen against who knew how many red alchemists and revenants. I was disgusted with myself for hoping they had tried to summon Anasztaz a few more times and failed, killing more and more of them.

But every time I thought they could have succeeded already, my stomach dropped. By Saint Sara-la-Kali, they couldn't summon the titan. They just couldn't.

Halfway through our trek, the sun set and dark enveloped us. I gathered a few branches from the forest ground and cast a magical flame on one of their ends, so they would act as torches.

When we got to the mine, we hesitated. There were no lights coming from the building anymore.

"What's going on?" Artan asked.

"They must have known we were coming," Theron said.

"How?" Kane asked.

"Either way, we have to go," Ramon said. "If they are hiding in there, we need to attack and stop them."

I nodded in agreement.

Slowly and quietly, we dropped our torches, surrounded the building, and waited for Theron's signal. Once he let out a short and loud whistle, we barged into the building by jumping through the broken windows and bursting through the doors.

Channeling my magic, I rushed, ready to stop the alchemists, or fight against a titan.

But the place was empty.

I glanced around at my friends standing around the room, all looking at each other, too stunned to move. The red blood circle was still drawn on the floor, lots of smears smudging the red lines, but the bowls with liquid were gone, and so were the alchemists and revenants.

"What happened?"

"Where are they?"

"Did they summon the titan?"

The questions flew through the building as we searched every corner, just to make sure our enemies weren't hiding, waiting for us to leave before they could keep trying to summon the titan—until they eventually succeeded.

"What's going on?" Artan asked, approaching Theron, Ramon, Kane, and me.

"I don't know," Ramon said, his voice tight.

"Do you think they succeeded?" Kane asked. "That they summoned the titan and left?"

I shrugged. "How would we tell?" We didn't know how the ritual was supposed to go, how the titan was supposed to look. What if it had killed all of our enemies when it was summoned, and now it was running through the forest, hunting for new victims?

"Come on." Theron beckoned to the main door right behind us. "Standing here won't help anything."

"I can shift and search the area," Ramon suggested as we walked out of the building. "If they left any scent or trail behind, I can find it."

"Are you sure about that?" I asked.

We halted and Ramon nodded. "I am."

"All right," Theron said. "But be back here in an hour. If you're not back, we'll go after you."

The other warriors gathered around us, but turned their faces when Ramon started stripping his clothes away—me included.

I only looked back at him after he shifted and let out a howl to let us know he was ready.

"Good luck," I whispered.

Then, he was gone.

And we stood there, waiting while he searched.

Not even five minutes later, Ramon was back. He shifted and put on pants.

"You won't believe what I found," Ramon said, out of breath.

"Tell us!" Theron said in urgency.

Ramon pointed to the broken mine elevator. "In there. There's a bunch of tziganes down there."

WE STARED AT HIM, STUNNED FOR A MOMENT.

"W-what?" Artan asked, taking a step back. For a moment, I thought he was drunk again, but it was just his shocked reaction.

"The tziganes left at Lovell when you fled," Ramon said. "I think they are down in the mine."

I gasped. "You smelled them?"

He nodded. "But I also smelled blood. I think some of them are hurt."

"What about the alchemists and revenants?" Kane asked.

"Didn't catch their scent," Ramon informed us.

"They are probably locked down there," I said. My heart squeezed. Those poor people.

"Then, we're going to rescue them right now," Theron ordered.

Our group rushed to the elevator opening. The elevator was gone, but the metal pillars that had once supported it were still there—rusty and bent, but there.

Artan looked down the elevator shaft. "How are we going to get down there and bring everyone up?"

An idea struck me. "Cora, it's earth down there. Can you create steps, like a winding stair around the elevator pit?"

"I think so," she said.

Standing at the edge of the pit, Cora closed her eyes and raised her arms. A moment passed and then the ground shifted. The first step jutted out from the pit wall. Then the second. Then the third.

I cast a small fire orb and dropped it in the pit. The orb flowed down with the creation of each new step, illuminating the way. Not that Cora needed it, since she could feel the earth, but I wanted to see her magic in action.

But soon the orb's glow wasn't enough and darkness reigned again.

"Just a little more," she whispered, focusing. "And ... done. There are steps all the way to the bottom."

Theron looked at us. "Ramon, Mirella, Kane, Artan, Cora, and Rye, come with me. The rest of you, watch the surroundings and help the tziganes who come up."

The warriors nodded in acknowledgment.

I conjured another orb of red flames and handed it to Theron. "It won't burn."

He took it and started down the steps. I conjured a few more orbs and gave them to Ramon and Cora. I kept my hand up with a flame in my palm.

Slowly, we made our way down the narrow steps—Theron in front, then me, Kane, Cora, Rye, Artan, and Ramon was last.

Afraid of taking a wrong step, I kept a shoulder against the wall of dirt to help me with balance. My anxiety flared up as we went down and down. I imagined that long pit caving in, trapping us, and it only made my breath shallower. The air grew thick, and despite the earth being cooler the lower we went, my hands sweated.

A long time later, Theron stopped moving.

"What is it?" I asked, extending my hands and projecting the glow of my flames wider.

The elevator was directly beneath him, broken and covering most the passage.

"We need to move it," Theron said. "Cora, come down here."

Cora created a few more steps so she could pass us, and

stood beside Theron. "I think I can move the earth here." She pointed to the last patch of earth before the opening. "That should loosen the wood of the elevator, then we can push it and it should move aside it easily."

"Why don't you just open a hole so we can pass?" Artan asked.

"Because I don't know the structure of this place," she said. "If I take too much earth out of one place, the entire thing might cave in."

"That's not good," Ramon said.

"Then, just do that," Theron said. "Move what you can, and we'll push and break through the elevator if necessary."

Cora focused and started moving the soil. The entire pit shook, and a little loose dirt fell over us, drawing grunts and groans from our group.

"Sorry," she said. After another push, the end of the pit was a little bigger. "That should do it."

Theron reached with his foot and kicked the board. It moved, but not enough. So, he sat down on the last step and jumped over the board. Even though I knew he wasn't far from the ground, my stomach tightened when he fell. The board broke in half when it touched the ground, but Theron was okay. He got up and dusted off his uniform. "It's all fine. Come down."

One by one, we jumped down on the broken board in the middle of the collapsed elevator.

I raised my hand, sending more of my fire light forward. The elevator shaft opened into a tunnel. It was as tall as a corridor in a house, but wider—and I still felt claustrophobic down here. There were a few abandoned metal wagons and rusty picks along the dirt walls.

Theron turned to Ramon. "Are you sure they are here?"

Ramon inhaled deeply. "Yes, their scent is stronger here."

"Let's find them and get out of here," Theron said. Raising the fire orb high, he marched forward, and we followed.

About a hundred yards ahead, the tunnel divided into five tunnels.

"Through there." Ramon pointed to the middle one.

We went ahead, everyone tense and holding their breath, as if we were expecting revenants and red alchemists to come jumping at us at any moment. Maybe they would. Ramon had said he hadn't smelled them down here, but we all knew our enemies had their foul tricks and could easily mask their scents.

Or they could have faked the tziganes' scent to bring us down here.

That thought chilled my blood.

I opened my mouth to say something about that when the end of the tunnel came into sight. Past the tunnel was a wide room. I molded the flames in my hand into a new, bigger orb, and sent it up, to illuminate the room. Red light shone around us. Tracks cut across the room and disappeared into smaller tunnels on each side. Several wooden doors lined the opposite wall, beyond the tracks.

"Where to?" Artan asked, looking side to side.

Ramon took a sniff. "They are close, very close."

"Anyone out there?" Theron shouted.

"Here!" a muffled voice came from behind one of the doors. "We're here! Help!"

Knocks rang through the doors, and voices grew louder.

We rushed forward and tried opening the doors, but they were locked.

Artan used his air power to turn the lock of one of the doors. Kane called on his power and his blades turned orange, cutting through the metal lock easily. I took one of the locks in my hand and melted it in no time.

The doors opened and tziganes spilled out, their faces and clothes dirty, their expressions haunted. They were pale and thin. My gut twisted as kids stumbled out, barely able to stand.

"By Saint Sara-la-Kali," Irene said in a mutter. She had worked at the infirmary in Lovell. "We're so glad you're here." She reached for us, but instead of embracing us, she pushed us back. "But we have to go, now."

"Yes, we should go," Milo insisted, his eyes wide. He had been one of the teachers in the Lovell school. "They will be back soon. We should go."

"They?" I asked, looking around the crowd that had gathered around us. They all looked not only like they were starving and weak, but also scared. Terrified. "They who?"

Irene shook her head. "You don't want to know. Let's just go, please."

She pushed us back again. Then, they all pushed us. A few of them didn't even wait for us, they started running toward the exit, in the dark.

What made them so scared that they were running without being able to see where they were going?

"Is it the red alchemists?" Cora asked.

"Or the revenants?" Rye asked.

"No," Milo said, his voice trembling. "Much worse." He grabbed my arm with his weak grip and tugged me. "Please, let's go."

I glanced at Kane and Theron, wondering what was going on?

"It doesn't matter," Theron finally said. "We got them. Now it's time to go."

Ramon nodded. "You're right. Let's help them out."

"Cora, take your orb and go to the front," Theron ordered. "Before the tziganes trip and crack their heads open."

I flinched at his words, but well, with all the picks and metal carts in the tunnels, that was a possibility.

Cora nodded once then dashed through the crowd, heading to the front. After a glance to Theron, Rye went with her.

"Next, the kids," I said, gesturing to come to me. I created another small orb and gave it to the oldest. "Follow our friend and you'll find the exit. There are more tziganes out there, waiting to help you. Okay?"

Holding tight to the orb, the oldest nodded then directed the kids to go with him.

"Now the elderly," Ramon said. A couple of older tziganes seemed like walking corpses. They wouldn't have the strength to walk out of here, much less to go up the stairs. "Artan, you take Clara. I'll take Martin."

Without complaining, Artan hooked his arms around Clara's legs and shoulders and picked her up. "I'll get you out of here."

"We should go," Irene repeated.

Theron looked around. "Anyone else out there?"

"I think we've got them all," Kane said.

Theron waited a few seconds. "All right. Let's go."

We headed toward the tunnel, but took only three steps before a horrible snarl echoed through the room.

"What's that?" I asked, the hairs on my arms standing on end.

"It's them," Irene said in a whimper. "Run!"

The guys and I didn't move for half a second, but then we saw them. Coming from the small tunnels on the sides, hunched shadows dragged their feet toward us. They made clicking and snarling sounds that reminded me of—

"Oh no," I muttered as my suspicions were confirmed.

Darcy, Oscar, Dika, and the other elder council members approached us—but they weren't themselves anymore. They were zombies, like Damara's undead army from before. She had turned them into undead and left them here to terrorize the other tziganes.

No, not for the other tziganes.

For us.

It had been a trap.

The tziganes were the bait, and we were the catch.

The first time I fought the zombie-tziganes, I had frozen. But this time, I knew. I knew they weren't themselves anymore. We could do nothing to save them.

I channeled my fire.

Beside me, Artan almost dropped Clara.

Shit, it was his grandmother and father coming for us, with their hunched backs, arms dangling, grayish skin, and glassy eyes.

And blood.

A lot of blood smeared their faces and hands.

My stomach curled.

"It's not them," I told him. I stepped in front of him, trying to draw his gaze away from the undead. "Artan, it's not them. You know this. You've seen this. You know they are gone."

He lowered his eyes at me, so full of anguish and pain. "It's ... I can't ..."

Despite everything, I felt an immense need to protect him, to comfort him. "Just go." I pushed him toward the tunnel. "Go with Ramon. Theron, take him."

"But the zombies," Theron protested.

"We'll take care of them," Kane said.

Theron dipped his chin in agreement before taking Artan's shoulder and pushing him and Clara away, with Ramon and Martin right behind them.

Kane and I positioned ourselves between the tunnel's opening and the incoming undead.

He drew out his twin swords. "Any plans?"

"Just wing it?" I said, because I didn't like the alternatives bouncing in my mind.

Zombie Vano was the first to reach us. Kane stepped forward and swung his swords in a cross in front of him, slicing Vano's throat. His body fell back, his head rolling away, as dark, dark red blood stained the dirt ground.

Bile rose to my throat, and I had to look away and take a deep breath before I threw up all over my feet.

But then Boldo and Dika were coming for us. Kane took down Dika in a similar manner, while I cast fire stakes and sent them at Boldo's chest. The stakes pierced his rotting flesh. Magically, they dove deeper until they disappeared inside his body. A moment later, Boldo started writhing and his gray skin turned orange as the fire spread inside him. Uttering groans and chilling clicking sounds, Boldo fell to his knees as his body turned red and his skin charred.

The rest of the elder council reached us, with Darcy and Oscar right in the middle.

Kane sliced through a zombie's chest. "To your left!"

I was finishing an undead, but quickly twisted, avoiding the other zombie's claws. I took a step back and assessed the situation. We could keep fighting, killing one by one, or we could end this in one blow—my original idea—and leave this place fast.

"Retreat," I told Kane.

He glanced at me, his eyes round. "Why?"

"Just do it."

Groaning, Kane took a few steps back. Channeling my magic, I raised my hands. Fire shot from the ground, right at the zombie's feet, enveloping their bodies. They shrieked and clawed and bit and stomped, trying to get away from the fire. Despite being surrounded by fire, the zombies kept coming, kept advancing.

Kane and I retreated a little more, watching them, waiting, hoping we didn't have to fight them anymore.

Some of the undead fell to the ground and didn't get up. Others, like Darcy and Oscar, were resilient. They didn't want to give up. Even while writhing and stumbling and their skin turning black, they advanced.

Kane and I took a few more steps back.

When Darcy's hands reached over the fire line, I was done with it. I raised my hands above my head, and the fire billowed, spreading through the entire room—from ground to ceiling, from side to side.

I held my breath, counting the seconds as Darcy fought against the fire consuming her. I thought the old hag would reach the border of the fire, but finally, she fell.

I waited and waited.

Kane put a hand on my shoulder, and I almost jumped out of my skin. "Sorry," he said, dropping his hand. I grabbed his hand in mine, not wanting him to think I didn't like him touching me. He squeezed my hand. "I think it's done."

I nodded. "I think so too."

Slowly, I walked back, toward the tunnel, my eyes on my fire, still expectant that one or more undead would jump out and lunge at us. But nothing happened. At the mouth of the tunnel, I brought my hands up, then down quickly. The fire was gone, as if it had been sucked out of the room from beneath.

Several bodies littered the dirt ground, unrecognizable.

These had been people we knew, people I had listened to, tried to obey and follow, people I had wanted to make proud. Even if their plan had been to torture and kill me, it still made me sick to see them all dead at my feet.

I turned to the wall, sank to my knees, and heaved. I hadn't eaten in hours and there was nothing for me to throw up, but I couldn't help it. Kane smoothed his hand on my back, saying it would all be okay.

Finally, after a few minutes, I stood on shaky legs. "I think I'm fine now."

My body was fine, meaning I wouldn't fake-throw up anymore. But my mind was messed up. Once more I had to kill, and this time it hadn't even been my enemies.

Kane slipped his hand in mine. "We better go. I'm kind of anxious to see if everything is okay outside the mine."

Shit, he was right. We had been fighting down here, but for all we knew, this was a trap, meaning there could be red alchemists and revenants attacking the rest of our group outside.

Together, we ran as fast as we could on the uneven ground. When we got to the broken elevator and steps, Theron and Ramon were still in the shaft, watching out for the last two rescued tziganes who were climbing up.

Theron turned to us. "I was going to give you two about five more minutes before I went back."

"Same here," Ramon said.

"We're fine," I told them. "It's done. They are all gone. For real this time." A sour taste coated my tongue. I hated saying that. And I hated that I would have to tell Artan and Ryane and the other tziganes that their family members had become zombies, and I killed them.

"Everything okay over here?" Kane asked, looking up. "No attacks from the top?"

Theron shook his head. "No. Everything is fine. It seems the red alchemists and revenants from before are gone."

I frowned. "What do we do now?" Though I deemed this mission a success because we had rescued the tziganes we thought we had lost, we had actually come here to stop the summoning of Anasztaz.

Ramon let out a long sigh. "I don't know."

"We should worry about our people first," Kane said.

"Right," Theron agreed. "They have been down here only Saint Sara-la-Kali knows for how long. They must be starving, dehydrated, and borderline sick. We need to take them to safety, then worry about our next step."

I nodded. "You're right."

The four of us went up the steps and exited the elevator shaft. Around us, my father, Cora, Rye, and the other warriors cared for the rescued tziganes, giving them water from their canteens, and simply comforting them.

They were right, I knew they were right, but as we made our way back to our camp, I couldn't help the pain cutting through my chest, telling me we shouldn't stop now. That we were making a mistake. We needed to go after Damara and her army and stop the summoning of the titan before it was too late.

I TRIED TO SLEEP. I EVEN CLOSED MY EYES AND STAYED IN THE tent with Kane for a few hours, but I couldn't relax. I felt exhausted but agitated, and no matter if I counted sheep or tried dreaming of angels, sleep didn't come.

When I dragged my feet out of the tent, careful not to wake up Kane, it was almost noon. The sun was warm, a gentle breeze brought the scent of wildflowers, and the birds sang loudly in the trees around the camp.

We had made it back to camp around four in the morning, mostly because we had to come slowly with the rescued tziganes. They were too weak to hike fast through the forest. And upon arriving, the entire camp woke up to greet the missing tziganes and take care of them.

The camp was still busy. Most rescued tziganes had been treated and fed and assigned to tents where they now rested. But there were a few still in the infirmary, because their dehydration or infections had been severe. The kitchen was also busy—my mother, my father and my grandmother worked on getting lunch ready for everyone.

Needing something to do to occupy my mind, I joined them.

The kitchen in the camp was rudimentary—we had bought a few gas tanks and standing cookers, but there was no oven. As for electricity, Clarita came a couple of times a day to zap the big freezer the guys had brought with her power. That was enough to keep it running smoothly.

By Saint Sara-la-Kali, how I missed our enclave.

I chopped the carrots for the creamy chicken soup that was on the menu as if I was getting my revenge on them.

"Slow down, Mirella, before you slice your finger off," my father said from my side, where he shredded the cooked chicken using two forks.

I paused. "Yeah, sorry."

He glanced at me. "No need to be sorry. Just be careful."

"I will," I muttered as I started chopping the carrots again, this time slower.

"Talk to me," he said, his voice low. "What's plaguing that mind?"

I pressed my lips tight. Before finding out I was a tzigane, and to be honest, until a few months ago, I had never talked about my problems and concerns with my mother. I had found out Dolan was my father about six months ago, and he was already trying to talk to me like she never did. What was his deal?

Realizing my stress and worry were seeping into my mood and making me a little hostile, I let out a long breath, exhaling all the negativity from inside. "The usual," I confessed.

"You mean Damara?"

I nodded. "Yes, and everything else. I can't stop my mind

from worrying about everything, even things that already happened and I can't change it."

"Like what?"

"Like ... killing the first undead tziganes, and last night, killing the zombiefied elder council. Losing Kizzy, and in a way, Trina too." I clicked my tongue. "I still can't believe she tried poisoning me, and even more shocking, that she's Damara's heart keeper." I dropped the knife and stared at the quiet tents dotting the camp. "And now there's this titan Anasztas. We don't know what happened. Did they summon him? Where is he? If they didn't, have they given up? Or did they move and are trying again? And—"

My father put a hand over mine. The words died on my lips. "Mirella," he started. "You're not alone. You never were and you never will be. We have the same worries as you do, and we'll do what we can to fix everything, I promise."

"I know, I know ... it's just, being here, chopping vegetables for a soup feels so unproductive."

"We have to feed our people," my father said. "Especially the ones we rescued last night. That's important too."

"I know, I know." I did know that. I wasn't stupid. Most of these people formed our army. How could we not worry about feeding them and keeping them strong? But still, I wanted to be out there, looking for Damara, fighting her. Ending this ~~for~~ once and for all.

"Don't be so harsh on yourself, Mirella. Everyone here loves you. Even when they might not agree with your decisions, they do love you."

Only because I was the beloved heart maiden. If I wasn't, then they would hate me. Hell, they would have banished me long ago. "If you say so," I muttered, unconvinced.

"He's right, you know," my mother whispered to my back as she walked past us.

"Mom!" I snapped.

"Don't yell at her," my grandmother said. She was standing in front of the cookers four feet behind us, starting the soup. "I happen to agree too."

I shook my head, but ended up smiling.

Thankfully, they were able to take my mind off it for a while. We talked about cooking and food and how the kids were enjoying the dance class from Ellie, as if we weren't living in a half-assed camp and facing another battle.

Lunchtime came and went. I helped them serve everyone, then cleaned up after everyone left.

It was early afternoon and we were talking about what to do for dinner when Kane showed up in the kitchen tent.

"Why didn't you wake me up?" he whispered to me.

Holding a pen and a notepad, I stood on my tiptoes and pressed a kiss to his lips. "Because you were sleeping so peacefully." Then, I turned to my father. "What do we have?"

"Not much." He looked around the tables and improvised shelves that made up our pantry. "Our numbers increased suddenly. We'll need to go grocery shopping tomorrow."

I frowned. Was this a good idea? Leaving the camp when we were in the midst of a war? What if Damara attacked while they were gone? Or worse, Anasztaz?

But food was a necessity. We had to buy groceries if we want to keep the tziganes strong.

"How about we worry about dinner first?" I walked to him and started looking around, trying to get ideas of what we could make for dinner.

"We might not have time for dinner tonight," Theron said.

I turned in the direction of his voice and found him on the other side of the table, his expression gloomy.

My stomach dropped. "What is it?"

"Urgent meeting at the main tent in five minutes," he said, before marching away.

I dropped the notepad and pen on the table and rushed to the main tent, with Kane and Dolan behind me. My mother and my grandmother arrived a couple of minutes later, probably after finding someone else to take over the kitchen.

Soon, the tent was busting with people—Theron, Ellie, Ramon, Violet, Artan, Ryane, Tomas, Cora, Rye, Leander, Lash, my mother, my father, my grandmother, Kane, and me.

Theron leaned over the table, pressing his palms on the open map. "Our scouts are back," he said, his voice as gloomy as his expression.

"And?" Artan asked. Again, he wasn't drunk. Perhaps he had turned a new leaf? It was hard to tell.

"Lovell is still occupied by alchemists and revenants, but no sign of Damara and Trina," Theron said. "However, we know where they are." I held my breath, knowing this wouldn't be good. "They are camped in a clearing halfway from Lovell to here. It seems they are gearing up and getting ready for something."

"You mean ..." my mother whispered.

Theron nodded. "Yes, we believe they are getting ready to march this way at nightfall."

Nightfall. That was only a few hours from now.

"So, what do we do?" Ellie asked.

Ryane spoke up, "We have too many sick and weak tziganes in the camp. We can't let them come here."

"I know that," Theron said. "And that's why I was going to

say, we need to get ready and meet them away from here."

"So, we hit them first," I said, not a question.

Theron nodded. "Yes. We gear up and go. No time to waste. The farther we are from here, the safer our people will be." He looked around the tent. "Everyone agree?"

We all nodded and said yes, our voices weak with apprehension and fear. It was happening; it was finally happening.

And I would face Damara for the last time.

"Do we have an actual plan?" Kane asked from beside me.

"Honestly, I don't think a plan will make a difference now," Theron said. "If we meet them halfway, they will probably be surprised to see us, and that will be our only advantage."

"You all worry about the army," I said, drawing everyone's attention to me. "Kane and I will worry about Damara and Trina."

Ramon narrowed his eyes at me. "Are you sure you can take them?"

"If they performed the fire flower ritual, they'll be as powerful as we are." I gestured to Kane and me. "We'll be the only ones able to stop them."

Theron nodded. "We'll distract the army, while you stop those two. Be as fast as you can so you can reduce the casualties."

My gut tightened. Casualties. There would be death, and not only on their side.

I really, really didn't like this.

"We'll try," Kane answered.

"Right." Theron looked down at the map as if it could contain some hidden message, some last minute secret that could save us. But it didn't. Nothing did. Finally, he lifted his eyes and puffed his chest. "Let's get ready for war."

16

Gathering an army and gearing up wasn't an easy and fast task. As much as we wanted to rush, we could only do so much. Almost an hour after the meeting had ended, we finally set out to where the scouts had seen Damara and her army camped.

My heart grew heavy with each step. We were leaving a bunch of sick and weak tziganes undefended, while heading to what was supposed to be the worse fight of our lives. Possibly our doom.

Theron and Ramon took the lead, while Kane and I were directly behind them. Dolan was to my right, and Cora and Rye were to Kane's left. Behind us, Artan marched with Leander and Lash. The rest of the warriors and Ramon's wolves, the ones strong enough for a fight of this scale, marched with us.

Thankfully, Ellie, Ryane, and Violet stayed back with my mother and my grandmother, to look over the elderly, kids, and other tziganes who couldn't join us. Felix and Vira begged me to come, but since we didn't have any other layer of protection, I asked them to stay behind as a last line of defense, in case we failed and Damara came for them. At least, I hoped Felix and Vira could distract them while the tziganes escaped.

Earlier, Theron had sent the scouts out again, to keep an eye on Damara, Trina, and their army, in case they started moving and came for us earlier than we thought.

Although, it didn't matter now. We were going after them and meeting them earlier than expected, and away from our camp.

As we marched, Theron turned tenser and tenser.

"What is it?" I asked, stepping to his side.

His brows curled down. "The scouts should be back by now."

That was not good. I opened my mouth to tell him that it didn't mean anything, that they were fine and just taking a longer route back, but I didn't want to hope too much. We weren't sure what happened, but right now, there was no reason to lie. Truth was: Damara wasn't an idiot. She had been alive for over two hundred years, and despite her madness, she was way too smart. If the scouts got too close, she would see them.

My blood soured.

Trying to be prepared, I sent out my senses. I doubted Damara would let me sense her, just as I wouldn't let her sense me, not anymore, but I had to try.

However, I came to a screeching halt when I sensed it.

"What is it?" Kane asked, stopping by my side.

In a matter of seconds, everyone had stopped.

"Mirella?" Theron asked, as if holding his breath.

"I can sense her," I said, astounded. It was as if she wanted me to sense her. "Damara and Trina and their entire army are a couple hundred yards in front of us." I pointed right ahead. "In a small clearing in that direction."

Gasps filled the air. Though everyone knew why we were here, it was quite different to actually see it. To actually face it. To be ready for a fight.

Theron pulled his sword from the scabbard at his sash. "Everyone, be ready."

The sounds of scratching metal echoed through the forest as the warriors drew their swords. At Theron's signal, we marched forward. No reason to be quiet now, since I was sure she knew we were coming. She knew we were close.

We emerged into the clearing where they were waiting for us. Damara with Trina by her side, standing right in the middle, with their army of red alchemists and revenants and undead filling half the clearing and disappearing behind the trees.

I swallowed as we halted about ten feet from her, forming a line of our own. Kane and I in the middle, Theron by my side, Ramon by Kane's. Our tziganes and wolves took their places behind us. We were visibly outnumbered, but I didn't let that intimidate me—not much. We were powerful, we were strong, we could do this.

We could kill Damara and Trina, get rid of their army, and start anew. An era of peace and prosperity and happiness.

That was my dream. That was what I was fighting for.

"I thought you weren't coming," Damara said, a teasing lilt to her voice. She looked regal in a long dark red dress that hugged her body, which was incredibly impractical for a fight. Her brown hair was tied in an intricate bun on top of her head, with a small red tiara around it. What, did she think she was queen of something? "I let your scouts tell you where we were, then killed them when they got back. So stupid, why did you send them back?"

My blood chilled. She really had killed them.

"I have nothing to say to you," I said, my voice loud and clear. "I'll give you one chance. Surrender now and we won't have to kill you."

She let out a laugh that sent goose bumps up my arms. "If you're not going to kill me, what are you planning to do? Put me back into one of those hidden rooms under the infirmary? *Nais tuke*, but I would rather die."

"Damara, it doesn't have to come to this," I insisted, promising myself it would be just this once. I wouldn't give her any more chances.

"It does!" she shouted, losing the laughter, the smile, the amused expression. "It does. I have to do this. I have to steal your powers and kill all of you. That's the only way to start again. To be reborn."

I frowned at her. "That's what you want? To get rid of us so you can be reborn?"

"So I can forget all the evil the tziganes inflicted on me, that you continue to inflict," she said. "Tziganes are envious and selfish people. They don't deserve to live. *You* don't deserve to live."

"She really has lost it," Kane whispered.

"I thought the heart keeper was supposed to push her madness away," Theron muttered. "Why didn't it work for her?"

"Perhaps she has been mad for so long, it can't suppress it," Ramon said.

It made sense, but it didn't matter right now. We could stand here arguing all day. We could say Damara and her army were evil, while they shouted we were the evil ones.

There would be no end to this.

But there would be.

Today.

"Nothing you say will change my mind." Damara extended her hands and flames covered her arms. "I'm here to kill you all and that's exactly what I plan to do."

She threw her arm forward, and a huge snake of fire launched at us. I quickly rose a wall of fire in its path. The fire from the snake joined the fire from the wall and I pulled them back, like a fire tornado that followed my magic.

Then, the battle exploded.

Kane went for Trina, while Theron, Ramon, and the others advanced on the red alchemists and revenants.

Damara hurled little shards of fire at me, making me dodge one side, then the other. Irritated, I cast a small shield of fire in front of my bent arm and used that to stop the shards.

"Isn't that a bit silly?"

"Silly? No, you mean fun," she said. A smile stretched over her lips. "Like this."

She flung a small spark to the ground. It exploded like a smoke bomb, spreading through the clearing like a dark shadow.

Coughing, I retreated a few steps. I kept my magic just under my fingertips, ready to react if she attacked.

A strong blow of wind chased the smoke away. I whipped my head to side and saw Artan, at the edge of the clearing, using his air power to cleanse the area.

"Where did they go?" Kane asked, lowering his swords.

"I don't know," I muttered, looking around. Damara and Trina had disappeared.

Distracted with trying to find Damara and Trina, I didn't

see the revenant jumping at me, until Kane swung his sword and cut its head off. Blood sprayed my legs and I cursed under my breath.

He engaged with other enemies surrounding us, while I stood my ground, still upset that Damara had gotten away so easily. That was her plan? To tease me but not confront me directly? How did she expect to kill me, then?

Straining my eyes, I looked around some more, expecting to find her at the edge of the clearing, seated in a throne like chair, cackling away as our people fought each other.

At one side, Artan used his wind power and sword skills to cut through the revenants and red alchemists. Cora and Rye were close to him, fighting in such a synchrony that it looked like they were dancing together. Ramon had wolfed out and was fighting alongside his pack. My father was near Ramon, brandishing his sword and killing our enemies.

But we had our loses too.

There were bodies everywhere on the ground—alchemists, revenants, and tziganes.

Terror paralyzed me as I witnessed when two red alchemists ganged up on Leander and cut through his chest with their shadow swords. Lash let out a terrible shout as he lunged on the alchemists. But a third one showed up from behind and slashed his back. Lash stumbled forward, right into another shadow sword.

"No," I whispered, feeling powerless.

Then, just a few feet behind me, Theron fought a red alchemist. A practiced warrior, Theron parried the alchemist's strike before twirling out of the way and bringing his sword out, cutting the alchemist's shoulder. The alchemist paused and hissed, giving Theron enough time to end it. He pierced his sword through the alchemist's stomach.

When he pulled it out, the body fell to his feet.

And a revenant who was just behind him jumped Theron. It bit Theron on the shoulder, and they tumbled to the ground.

"Theron!" I screamed, sending a fireball at the revenant. The fireball weaved through the people between us, and exploded against the revenant's back. The vampire-like monster shrieked as my fire spread and burned him to a crisp.

Theron crawled from under him, his hand on his shoulder.

I rushed to my brother and knelt beside him. "Are you okay?"

He hissed. "It stings."

I pried his fingers from his shoulder, hoping I had seen wrong. But I hadn't. The revenant had bitten him. "You need to get back to the camp."

"No, I'm going to fight!" The bite had already infected him —his face was pale, he was drenched in sweat, and his hands shook.

"You can't, not like this."

"Here." Our father knelt beside us. "I'll take him," he assured.

"No," Theron protested.

"Don't argue with me, boy," our father said, his voice rougher and stronger than usual. "Now go," he told me. "Find Damara. End this."

I glanced at Theron. I knew how it hurt him to stay back while the fight was going on. "I'm sorry." I patted my father's hand, then jumped to my feet, and after slaying two revenants, I went back to Kane's side.

"Where were you?" he asked, after killing a red alchemist.

I shook my head. "I'm going to look for Damara."

"I'm going with you," he said.

With no idea where to go, Kane and I weaved through the crowd, bringing down any red alchemist or revenant who stepped in our path. We made our way to the edge of the clearing, then went around its perimeter, always looking, but there was no sign of Damara and Trina.

A revenant jumped an injured tzigane by us, but Kane was faster. He kicked the creature aside, then slashed his swords, cutting through the vampire's abdomen.

"*N-nais tuke*," the young warrior said, clearly scared.

Rage and agony swam with the magic in my blood. Because of them ... because of Damara's evil plans, so many tziganes had lost their lives, and so many more were injured.

This fight ... it seemed so pointless.

"I can't find her," I muttered, disappointed. I needed to end this now.

"Then, we should focus on helping the others," Kane suggested. "Kill the red alchemists and revenants in this clearing and thin out her army. She'll be weaker without them."

Would she? They seemed to be cannon fodder.

I opened my mouth to agree when her laughter reached my ears.

I whirled on my heels.

There she was, standing at the edge of the forest, with Trina by her side, and a young warrior in her hands. Her eyes on mine, she sent her magic into the warrior.

"No!" I cried.

The warrior screamed as her fire burned him from the inside out.

I ran to her, to him, but it was too late.

She dropped him like a rag doll. Smiling at me, she turned and ran. Trina went with her.

To my surprise, all our enemies stopped fighting and followed Damara and Trina.

"What the fuck?" Kane asked.

Oh, they wouldn't escape so easily.

"After them!" I shouted, hoping my people heard me.

Kane and I followed, heading toward the unknown.

17

———

THE RUSH THROUGH THE FOREST DIDN'T LAST LONG. BEING supernatural creatures, the revenants outran us, and the red alchemists used some kind of trick. Still, we didn't stop following their tracks.

Artan caught up with Kane and me. "We're heading toward the other clearing, the ones the scouts said they saw Damara and her army in prior to the battle."

"Are you sure?" I asked, out of breath. Running and speaking wasn't my thing.

"Yes, Theron pointed it out on the map." Slowing down a bit, Artan looked around. "Where's Theron?"

My heart clenched. Theron had been bitten by a revenant. I knew the effects of that weren't good, but I didn't know to what extent. And that worried me way too much.

"He was injured," Kane answered.

"Shit." Artan frowned. "We're getting close."

We slowed down. Assuming Theron's role, Kane raised his hand, his fist closed. My father, Cora, Rye, Jayme, the other warriors, Ramon, and his wolves slowed down.

A jolt of magic brushed against my skin. "I can feel something," I whispered, walking forward.

We paused at the edge of the clearing, staying behind the tree line, and watched out. Damara and Trina stood near the center of the clearing, revenants around them. Just a few feet from them, red alchemists placed bowls on the ground.

I gasped. "No!" I rushed forward, to do what, I didn't know. To stop them? To burn the ground and destroy the damn bowls? To kill the alchemists?

But three steps later, I hit an invisible wall and fell backward. Pain ricocheted through my back as the air flew from my lungs. My head spun.

"Mirella!" Kane caught my arm and tugged me up. "Are you okay?"

No, I wasn't. I regained my footing and fought through my blurred sight. I reached forward with my hand, but I didn't touch it. The air shimmered with orange where the shield was located.

Damara had locked us out.

While she summoned Anasztaz.

Having noticed the commotion, the alchemists paused the organization of the ritual, but Damara urged them to keep going. Clearly amused, she smiled at me.

If only I could slap some sense into her.

"Damara, don't be an idiot," I cried. "Stop this ritual. You can't control the titan."

She either couldn't hear me, or she simply ignored me—I was opting for the latter.

"What do we do now?" Cora asked.

"Try opening a passage that goes under the shield," Kane suggested.

"Good idea," Rye agreed.

Hands like claws, Cora move her arms apart. The earth shook and a small hole appeared in the ground a foot from us. Groaning, Cora expanded the hole, pushing it under the shield. When the grass turned to dirt and the opening of the passage showed up on the other side, Cora dropped low and spied inside the small tunnel she created.

Brows furrowed, she pulled back and stood. "It's there. The shield. It's cutting through the passage."

"By Saint Sara-la-Kali," I muttered.

In the clearing, the alchemists had finished setting it for the ritual. They stood on the perimeter of the blood-drawn circle, with Damara several feet behind them.

"They're starting," Kane said, his voice urgent.

Channeling my power, I stepped back. With all I had, I let my magic out. A stream of fire burst from my hands and hit the shield. The shield shimmered orange, cracking, but it didn't break.

The alchemists chanted.

I inhaled deeply and tried again. This time, I held on longer and threw in as much of my power as I could. I could sense my magic well, and even with the increased power from the fire flower, it would be depleted soon. I couldn't sustain it for long.

But I had to try. By Saint Sara-la-Kali, I had to try. I had to succeed.

The ground shook underneath us.

I dropped my magic as an invisible magic exploded from the circle in the clearing, sending several red alchemists and revenants flying. A form started taking shape, its figure shimmering at first, but as it transformed, it grew dark.

A monster over twenty feet high appeared in the middle of the blood circle. Long, dark limbs and a thick chest resembling pieces of rock glued together, white lines running between the rocks, like a bright river. The monster turned its dark head around.

"What do we have here?" it asked, its voice rough and deep.

I winced with fear.

Its mouth was a huge hole that could devour one of us with a single gulp, and its big eyes seemed like two shining white rocks.

The monster roared. My ears rang and a chill ran down my spine.

Anasztaz was here. The titan had been summoned.

What the hell were we supposed to do now?

"Anasztaz," Damara said, her voice loud. "Hear me." Snarling, the monster turned to her. "I'm your summoner. I've freed you from the underworld. Now, obey me. Do my bidding."

In response, Anasztaz let out another roar. "You puny tzigane." The titan swiped his rocky hand toward Damara, clearly trying to get her.

The heart maiden jumped back, startled. "I order you to obey me!" She pointed to us. "Get them! Eat them! Kill them!"

Anasztaz didn't hear her. It swung its hand again, grabbing one of the alchemists cowering on the side. As if it were an appetizer, the titan popped the alchemists in its big mouth and chewed.

My stomach revolved.

"Do something!" Trina yelled.

"I'm trying!" Damara called her fire and sent it at Anasztaz. A thick snake of fire twisted up around the titan's body, caging him in like a rope. "You're mine, Anasztaz! Do my bidding!"

"You can't stop me." With a chilling roar, the monster broke free from the fire snake and reached for Damara again. She dodged its big hand, and it caught another alchemist on the way.

And again, he shoved the alchemist inside its mouth.

When things seemed they couldn't get any worse, small holes opened in the ground around the titan and what I supposed were its fiends popped up—miniature versions of Anasztaz, but still three heads taller than an average person.

"Bring them to me!" shouted the titan to its fiends.

The fiends were much faster than their master, and they advanced on the red alchemists and revenants without mercy. Screams echoed from the clearing, and I buried my head into Kane's arm, not wanting to witness the terror.

A crackling sound startled me.

"The shield," Cora said, surprised.

I looked up as the shield around the clearing shimmered and cracked. Beyond the shield, Damara fought against Anasztaz, trying to push him back, while still trying to control him.

Because of her distraction, the shield was breaking.

"Push it," I said. "If you have magic, use it against it. It'll break."

Cora threw rocks at it, Artan blew his wind, and I sent my fire.

The shield came down.

"Mirella," my father started. "There's nothing we can do now. We should retreat."

"Retreat?" I asked, confused. "If we retreated, Anasztaz will kill everyone here, and then he'll come after us. We'll have to fight it, no matter what."

"But we don't know how to stop it," Artan said. "We should retreat and find another solution."

I chewed the inside of my lip. I knew they were right, but it killed me to see the red alchemists and even the revenants being killed like flies on the wall by the titan and its fiends.

Sometimes, I hated being so soft-hearted.

"Right," I muttered, practically forcing the word out. "You're right."

I inhaled deeply and opened my mouth to order everyone to retreat, when the ground started shaking again. Stronger this time, more violent.

"What's going on?" Kane asked, reaching for me. We used each other to keep our balance, but instead of stopping, the ground shook more.

"I can feel it," Cora said, looking to the center of the clearing. "The holes in the ground. They are opening."

"What do you mean?" I asked.

"The ground is caving in," she said. "But I think I can stop it."

She rushed forward.

"Cora, no!" Rye shouted, running after her.

We all ran after her.

The holes in the ground continued to grow, the pit kept widening, creating a crater in the center of the clearing. Red alchemists, revenants, and fiends fell into the abyss.

"Wait," I said, holding back. "Don't stop it yet." I pointed to the other side of the widening pit.

Anasztaz was at the edge. The pit expanded a little more, and the titan lost its balance. Slowly, he slipped down the hole.

But not before swiping his hand and grabbing Trina.

"Noooo!" Damara shouted, a scream that chilled my bones.

"Now," Cora said, aiming her hands toward the pit, which continued to advance.

"Cora," I called her, not liking this.

"Stay back," she said through gritted teeth. "I can do this."

She groaned, infusing her magic in the earth.

The speed of the expansion slowed, and I thought, I hoped, it would stop. But it didn't.

In the blink of an eye, it sped up again, advancing toward us with a vengeance.

Taking Cora with it.

Making my heart stop.

Tearing a spine-chilling scream from Rye.

I stared at Cora, at her terrified face as she disappeared into the fissure.

18

THE NEXT FEW SECONDS WERE BOTH A RUSH AND IN SLOW motion. In shock, I couldn't move. Kane grabbed my arm and pulled me back before I was swallowed by the pit, which kept growing, kept eating the earth and everyone in its way.

We were deep into the trees when we finally stopped. Holding our breath, we waited for it, for the earth to tremble beneath our feet and advance toward us.

But it didn't. The crater had stopped, its edge a few yards from us.

Kane pulled me to him. "Are you okay?"

No, I wasn't okay. Leander and Lash were gone, Theron had been bitten by a revenant, and Cora had been swallowed alive.

Pain and agony filled my chest, making it hard to breathe, to think. All I wanted was to curl into a ball and cry. And give up.

Rye's screams cut through the fog in my mind, but only added to my pain. He fought against Jayme and Artan, who held him back. I was certain that if the guys let him go, he would jump headfirst into the crater and not look back.

I tried to think through the pain, I tried coming up with a plan, but there was nothing there. I couldn't think of one single thing.

"We should retreat," my father suggested, his voice low. "We have lost too many, their side is in chaos too, and we have no idea what just happened."

Kane nodded. "We need to retreat and regroup."

Not to mention take the dead back to camp and treat the injured before it was too late.

"Right," I muttered.

In his wolf form, Ramon rushed to me. I hadn't even noticed he had been gone, and even so, a wave of relief hit me knowing he was okay.

He nudged his muzzle on my leg and jerked his head.

I frowned. "You want me to follow you?"

He nodded.

I went with him, closer to the crater. He stopped at the edge and let out a yelp, his eyes fixed ahead. I followed his gaze and found what he wanted to show me.

Damara, knelt at the edge of the pit, crying for Trina.

A rush of rage and disgust washed over me.

I channeled my power and, skirting the crater, ran to her. I threw a jet of fire at her. "You crazy bitch!" She didn't resist it. She let the fire hit her and push her back. Tears streaming down her face, she curled on the ground. "I warned you. I told you no one could control the titan." I stepped closer. "Now Trina is gone, along with my friends."

A sob cut through her throat. "By Saint Sara-la-Kali, Trina ..."

Was she kidding me? I cast a snake of fire that twisted

around her body. It propped her up, sitting her on the ground, then it tied her ankles and her wrists behind her back. I infused as much power as I could into the magical fire ropes, afraid that she could break free of them if she tried.

"What are you going to do now? Resurrect Trina? Let me see you try!"

Damara finally lifted her red eyes to me. "I need to rescue her."

I stared at her. "Rescue? You mean ... you think Trina is alive?"

"She should be." She sniffed. "When the titan fell, it must have gone to the underworld. Trina is probably there with it."

I frowned. "Even if Trina didn't die when she fell into the pit, the titan devours tziganes. Who says it hasn't eaten her already?"

She flinched. "Because we brought it up before. It'll probably hold on to her and the others who fell with him, as a bargaining chip, to have us bring it back."

So ... she meant, Cora could still be alive too? Unwelcome hope invaded my chest.

I sent another snake of fire to her. It twisted around her body and helped her up, before tying it around her chest and arms. "You're coming with me."

<hr>

As I expected, my father, Kane, Artan, Jayme, and Ramon protested my idea. Rye tried to jump on Damara many times, but I assured him he didn't want to hurt her yet.

The sun was rising when we made our way back to the camp. The tziganes were either shocked by Damara dragging her feet behind me, or saddened by our numbers. Half of us were gone, and a quarter was injured. The infirmary became full and busy in no time. I got a glimpse of Theron lying on a bedroll, clearly sedated. I couldn't help worrying about him, about what would happen to him, but for now, I would leave him in Ryane's hands and the other more experienced tziganes.

Worried about the fact that she wasn't resisting me, I pulled Damara into the main tent and pushed her into a chair—the fire ropes still tight around her.

Kane stood by my side, quiet and tense, probably opposing whatever I was doing, but I couldn't help it. If there was a chance …

I shook my head, trying not to get ahead of myself here.

The others soon filed in the tent—my mother, my father, my grandmother, Artan, and Jayme. Ellie showed up, too, with Rye, who seemed like a walking body.

"I gave him something to calm down," she explained.

Lastly, in his human form and fully dressed, Ramon came in.

A pang cut through my chest when I looked around the table. Our numbers were reducing and I hated it. I loathed it.

"Are you going to share with us why this—?" Artan pressed his lips tight. "Why is she here?"

"Damara thinks Trina and Cora and whoever else fell into the pit are alive," I told them. They all gasped.

"Is it true?"

"By Saint Sara-la-Kali."

"We need to go there now."

Rye glared at Damara. "How do you know we can trust her?"

I let out a sigh. "I don't trust her, but I can feel her pain. She's suffering because of Trina's loss, just as much as you are for Cora." He winced. "If there's a chance Cora and the others are alive down there, we need to find out."

Dolan shook his head. "So, you're planning on storming wherever the titan is? No plan to detain it after that?"

I wished I had a better answer. "According to Damara, the titan is in the underworld, because apparently, that was his home before being imprisoned."

"But ... how?" my grandmother asked, as confused as I was.

"The titan can't get out of the underworld, but it can go there at any time," Damara said, her voice slow and slurred, as if she was drunk. "Instead of being trapped in a hole in the ground, it must have gone back to the underworld."

Everyone tensed. I wasn't sure if it was because Damara had spoken up, or because her answer wasn't the best one.

"Underworld," Kane muttered. "How do we get there?"

"There are ways," Damara said simply.

"What does it matter if we can get there, if we can't stop the titan?" Artan asked. "Even if it can't follow us out of the underworld, we'll still need to face it to rescue everyone."

"Right," Kane said. I stared at him. Was he agreeing with Artan? Hell was freezing over. "If we don't find a way to stop Anasztaz, we all will perish there."

"I might know a way," Damara said, sounding more focused. Although her face and eyes were still red, she wasn't crying anymore.

Dolan crossed his arms. "How?"

"Well ... I don't know how, but I know where to find out how," she clarified.

"Here we go," Artan said. "She'll spin a crazy tale, and when we realize it, we'll be caught in her web. Then she'll kill us."

I frowned. I didn't want to dismiss Artan's warning, but something made me believe Damara right now. Trina was her heart keeper. If Kane were missing, I would be going crazy. I would do anything. I would help my enemies. I would give away my soul, my life, to rescue him. I wouldn't dare play a game.

I looked at Kane, standing right by my side, my shoulder touching his arm. I loved him way too much.

That was how I knew Damara wasn't lying.

"Tell us," I said.

Damara straightened in her chair. "The secret room in the Lovell library. You know which one; I sent you there." I nodded and she went on, "There are other records there, more secrets the elder council tried to hide, and I'm sure there's a book about Anasztaz in there."

"Wait," Ramon started. "You're telling us to go to Lovell, which because of you is crawling with red alchemists and revenants right now. Is that right?"

"Moreover, about this book," Rye said. "How are you sure? Have you seen it?"

Even tied with fire ropes and under heavy glares, Damara didn't lose her composure. "No, I haven't, but I've seen others like it, with secrets and spells and how-tos and other crazy things you can't even imagine. I've also seen books on monsters and creatures in there. I haven't read all of them, but I'm *sure* there's one about Anasztaz."

"Do you believe her?" my mother asked me.

Once more, I thought of Kane and how I would do anything for him. I nodded. "I do."

Artan cursed under his breath. Ramon shook his head.

"It's possible," Sheila said. The tent went silent.

"What do you mean, *puri daj*?" I asked.

"Though I was never a Lovell tzigane, I was friends with many who were," my grandmother said. "I heard from a deceased elder council member about the secret section in the library, though I have no idea where exactly it is or how to access it. She said that there were books in there that nobody would ever believe were true." She glanced at me. "You've been there to read a book nobody knew existed. So, if you think this could be true now too, I'll support you."

I felt Kane's hand on my back—the support and encouragement I needed.

"I'm going," I said, looking around at everyone. "I can't simply sit here and hope for the best, but I'm not going to force anyone to come with me. We know this is a wild goose chase, that we may get to the secret library and not find a book about the titan, but I have to try. So ... if you want to come with me, say so."

Rye was the first one to speak up. "I'm in."

"If you go, I go," Ramon said, looking at me.

Artan groaned. "Me too."

"I'll go," Jayme said.

"I'll go too," Sheila said.

I stared at her. "*Puri daj!*"

"I'm old, but I can be useful." She winked at me.

"*Daj*, stay here and I'll go," my father said.

My grandmother took my father's hands in hers. "This time, you stay and watch over the camp, while I go out on an adventure with my beloved *puri chey*."

I didn't like it, but she was my grandmother, meaning she was as stubborn as I was. Nobody would change her mind now.

"All right," I said with a sigh. "We'll be leaving in thirty minutes."

"Mirella!" my mother snapped. "You just came back after being out all night. You need to rest." She looked around at everyone and I did the same. Disheveled hair, gaunt faces, pale skin, dirty and bloody clothes. If I looked half as bad as they did, I understood her concern. "You all do."

"But—"

"No buts," she cut me off. "If Damara says Anasztaz will use Cora and Trina and the others as bait, he won't kill them in one hour or ten. So, please, just wash up and rest for a few hours." Her brows knotted. "Don't make me order you."

One corner of my lips tugged up in amusement. As if she could order me around. But I understood her point, and I could see how terrible everyone looked. I could only imagine how tired they felt.

"All right," I said, giving in. "Meet me back here at sundown. Tonight, we invade Lovell."

19

I ATE, WASHED UP, AND THEN CURLED UP WITH KANE IN HIS tent to sleep. But, like the last time I tried to rest, sleep didn't come easily, and when it came, it was filled with nightmares.

I dreamed about Leander and Lash dying and coming back as ghosts to haunt me. About Theron becoming a revenant and attacking everyone in the camp. About Trina being buried under the earth and dying alone. About Damara betraying us—taking us to Lovell and handing us over to the red alchemists and revenants, while laughing that she had finally succeeded.

After the last one, I found I couldn't sleep anymore.

Kane got up with me. "We should eat something before getting ready," he suggested as we walked out of his tent, our hands linked.

Agreeing, we went directly to the kitchen tent, where we grabbed coffee and some store bought cinnamon muffins. My mother and father were there, already working on dinner for later.

I bit down on my muffin, then stared at it. "How's Damara?"

"Last time I checked, she was sleeping," my father said.

I had put Damara in a small tent by herself, with plenty of warriors to watch over her. Because of the situation, I doubted she would try to run, but one could never be too safe.

I grabbed another muffin and cup of coffee. "Be right back."

Kane didn't follow me as I went to Damara's tent. The warriors saw me approaching and stepped aside, letting me pass. I bent down to pass through the opening flap, then knelt beside the mattress in the short tent.

Damara was lying on the mattress, her ankles and wrists still tied with my fire rope. I frowned, suddenly upset that I had let her go to bed with her clothes still dirty and smeared with blood.

She might be my enemy, but I wasn't that heartless.

Like me, Damara was having nightmares. Forehead damp with sweat, she trembled and muttered nonsense, visibly scared.

With a loud gasp, she sat up and stared at me with wide eyes. "By Saint Sara-la-Kali."

"Nightmare?"

"Many." She let out a long breath, trying to calm down. "What time is it? You haven't gone to the library yet, have you?"

"No, not yet." In my mind, I wished the ropes around her wrist away. They disappeared a moment later. She rubbed at her reddened wrists. "Here." I offered her the coffee and the muffin.

She eyed them suspiciously. "I'm assuming there's no poison in them."

"It pains me to say, but right now, we're on the same side. So no, there's no poison in them." I brought them up, near my lips. "If you want I can take a sip and take a bite to prove it to you."

She tsked and took the coffee and muffin from me. "It pains me to say it, but I believe you."

"I'll have someone bring you something to wash up and clean clothes." I started retreating.

"Mirella, wait." One of Damara's hands shot up and she grabbed my wrist. I watched her, ready to whip her ass if she tried anything funny. "Take me with you. To the library. I want to help. I *need* to help."

I shook my head. "The others won't like it."

"I know." Her eyes filled with tears. "But I can't stay here and count the seconds, waiting for you to return. You know ..." She pressed her hand to her chest. "You know how I feel about Trina. You feel the same way about Kane. Imagine if you had to sit out while everyone else went to save him." Her voice broke. "I can't bear it."

Why, oh why was I sympathizing with the enemy? I shouldn't care about what she said, I shouldn't care about what she felt. She had almost killed me several times. Because of her, many of my friends were dead. Because of her, I had to kill people.

Yet, I felt for her. She was a broken woman. She had been tortured and abused by the elder council long ago. She had lost her first heart keeper—a pain I couldn't begin to understand. And now she was about to lose her second heart keeper—her second chance.

Unlike her, I wasn't evil. I could show her how to be a proper heart maiden, a better person.

I doubted she cared, but it had to start somewhere, right?

"All right," I whispered. "I'll let you come with us."

A tear rolled down her cheeks. "*Nais tuke.*"

I wished I still carried my old smartphone around, so I could have recorded that, because Damara saying thank you? That was worth millions.

A couple of hours later, right before sundown, we met in the main tent. Kane, Ramon, Artan, Rye, Jayme, Sheila, and I —everyone rested, fed, and geared up.

And Damara.

Because I didn't trust her entirely, I had left strong fire bindings around her wrists, but other than that, she was free.

"What is she doing here?" Rye asked, venom in his words. I was sure he wouldn't hesitate to kill Damara, if she wasn't our only hope of finding Cora and the others again.

"She's going with us," I said. Many protests started. "No!" I practically shouted. "I don't want to waste time arguing about this. Damara is coming and that's it. If you don't agree, then please, sit this one out." No one uttered a peep. "All right, then if everyone is ready, let's go."

THE TREK TO LOVELL DIDN'T TAKE LONG. THE ENCLAVE WAS eerily dark as we approached it through one of the side gates.

"Shouldn't it be full of red alchemists and revenants?" Kane asked, as we watched the gates in the distance from behind trees.

"Didn't you leave them here, so we couldn't come back?" I

asked Damara directly. No time to play games now. I would ask direct questions and expected direct answers.

"I did," she said, sounding confused. "There should be a few of them around the gates, even if the interior wasn't too full." She stared straight into my eyes. "So you would think it was."

I exhaled sharply. "All right. We're going in slowly and hiding in the shadows. If we see anyone, we hide if we can. If we can't ... we fight our way to the library. If we can get in and barricade it, we should have time to find the records before they swarm in."

"Sounds like a plan," Rye said, eager to go into the enclave.

Practically tiptoeing, we went to the gates. They were locked, but we easily broke the lock and entered the enclave. The inside was as dark and eerie as the outside. And empty too. As we advanced toward the library, we didn't see one red alchemist or revenant. Not one living soul.

Even so, we closed the library doors after we went in, and locked them.

Ramon said, "Jayme and I will stay here, to watch over the door. If we see something, we'll let you know right away."

I nodded and advanced through the row of shelves toward the back of the library. It was utterly dark in here, but I didn't dare call my fire, not yet, in case our enemies were hiding and saw it.

In the back, I walked into a square formed by tall book-shelves, lined with the back wall and the wall from the main administrative building beside the library.

This time, I didn't hesitate. I went to the corner, where the walls met, most of the space hidden by the tall shelves along the walls. I placed my hand in the same spot as before and imagined the lock opening and the wall shrinking behind the shelf. A faint *click* sounded and the wall moved to the side, showing a doorway.

"Wow," Artan whispered.

Conjuring an orb of fire in my hand, I stepped into the secret room.

It was just as I remembered with a long wooden table in the middle and several shelves filled with leather-bound books, scrolls, and loose paper around it.

Sheila looked around, her eyes wide. "This is incredible."

I turned to Damara. "Which shelf?"

Damara turned to the left. "This one." She halted in front of a tall shelf with ledgers and thick stacks of paper tied together with thin leather laces. "Last time I was in here, many, many years ago, I found the books on monsters and other supernaturals on this shelf."

I let out a sigh. "All right. Let's grab the books and search through them."

I pushed my orb up, making it float over the room, to illuminate the shelf, then I conjured a few more, since the room was way too dark. I reached for as many books as my arms could carry.

In no time, the wooden table in the center of the secret room was crammed with books and paper, and all of us skimmed through them, searching for the titan who had taken our friends.

Damara helped, even though her hands were bound. She kept shooting me glances, as if I would be stupid enough to let her totally free, but she didn't complain and resumed her reading.

About an hour and many books later, Rye cried, "Here! I found it!"

A sense of relief flooded me. By Saint Sara-la-Kali, I had been so tense and scared that we wouldn't find anything, my stomach had been tight and my breath heavy since we started this mission.

Now, I just hoped we found something that made sense and we could use it, then I would breathe easier.

I leaned over Rye's shoulder and read the entry on the book.

"What does it say?" Sheila sked from the other side of the table.

"It says …" Rye shook his head. He flipped through the pages, searching for more, but Anasztaz's entry was short and not helpful. "It says the only way to send the titan back to its prison or kill it is to use the Stone of the Tziganes."

"Stone of the Tziganes?" Artan asked. "What's that?"

"I don't know," Sheila whispered.

I glanced at Damara.

"Don't look at me," she said, raising her arms. "I don't know either."

"There has to be something about the stone in a book in this secret library," I said, looking at the shelves. "Start looking."

We moved away from the table as Ramon and Jayme ran into the room.

"Alchemists," Ramon said urgently. "Alchemists are coming this way."

We all formed a line in front of the table, including Damara, and waited for them.

When the alchemists stepped into the secret room, I cast flames in my hands. "Stay where you are if you don't want to be burned alive."

One of the alchemists took off his mask and raised his hands. "We're not here to fight."

That caught me by surprise, but I didn't lower my guard. "W-what?"

"My name is Allen, and I'm the new leader of the alchemists in Lovell. Fiends from Anasztaz showed up and took several of us down to the underworld, including our leader, Holden."

"Why should we care about that?" Kane asked, his tone hard. I knew he was trying to intimidate them, in case they were trying to trick us.

"Because we're more loyal than you think," Allen said. "Even if you don't agree with our culture, I know you care about honor and loyalty." He gestured to the ten alchemists behind him. "We're all that's left in the enclave. Even the revenants fled, afraid of the fiends."

"Do you know them?" I asked Damara in a low voice. "Aren't they your men?"

"I ordered them around; I didn't really know them," she whispered. "I don't know their names or ranking, or whatever."

That was helpful.

I braced myself before asking, "What do you want with us?"

"We want to help you," Allen said. "If we don't team up to stop Anasztaz, we'll all be dragged down to the underworld with him. We'll all be exterminated."

I flinched with his visuals, but I couldn't deny he had a point.

"Even if we were to believe you, there isn't much we can do to stop the titan," Rye said, his voice clear that he was frustrated.

"Tell them," Damara said to me. "About the stone. Tell them. If you don't, I will."

I frowned, suspicious of her doings, as usual. Without much choice, I relented. "We might be able to stop Anasztaz with the Stone of the Tziganes."

"Why did you tell him that?" Artan hissed at me.

"Then all is not lost," Allen said.

"What do you mean?" Kane asked.

"We know where the Stone of the Tziganes is."

I waited for a sly grin, a glint of amusement in his dark eyes, but there was nothing. The alchemist was serious.

"That's too good to be true," Rye said.

It was, but if they really knew about it ... "I don't trust you," I said. "You could be playing a trick here."

Just like the others said Damara was. Deep in my gut, I knew Damara wasn't, but the red alchemists were different. Even though they had lost their peers, it wasn't like the heart maiden losing her heart keeper. This time was different, and I wouldn't trust them easily.

"I can prove we're on your side," Allen said. "We can make a potion together that binds our word to you. We'll promise to stop hunting all tziganes if you let us help you destroy Anasztaz."

My brows furrowed. "What happens if you don't keep your promise?"

"We'll die," he said, deadpan. "Instantly."

"You can't buy that," Artan whispered.

"It's the only chance we have," Kane objected.

I looked at Damara and asked in a low voice, "Do they really have the stone?"

"I think so," she said. "I heard rumors about it. If someone knows its location, it's them."

I didn't like it. I didn't like any part of this whole thing.

Could we please go back to a normal world without magic and tziganes and enclaves and magical powers and heart flowers?

I let out a long breath.

"If you're thinking about accepting," my grandmother started. "I can help. I can do the potion for them. That way we'll be sure the potion is right, and they will keep their word."

"You can do that?"

She nodded. "I might not be a specialist in potions like Cianna was, but I know my way around it just fine." My heart tugged. Cianna was my other grandmother, my mother's mother, who had died at the hands of Damara.

So many reasons to hate her, and yet, right now, I felt only pity for her.

"All right," I said, cutting through the chatter around me. "We'll do it, but only if Sheila can do the potion and you drink it." I gestured to my grandmother.

Allen didn't hesitate. "Deal."

20

"It's too good to be true," I whispered.

Kane held my hand tight. "I think so too, but I'm trying to believe."

With a sigh, I looked out the SUV's window, at the dark road ahead of us.

After agreeing to the deal, we all, including the red alchemists, had followed Sheila to the elixir-making room in the main building, where she concocted the potion that would bind the alchemists' words to me. Without hesitation, they drank the potion and promised to not hurt a single tzigane while helping us, otherwise they would die an instant and painful death.

Then, they told us the Stone of the Tziganes was in one of the hideouts in a nice neighborhood of Broken Hill, the small town I used to live in before becoming the heart maiden.

Still suspicious, we got an SUV and a van from the enclave's garage and drove toward the town. We followed them into a nice subdivision and into the driveway of a fancy house on a cul-de-sac.

I shuddered, remembering when Ellie had been enchanted by the alchemists and took me to a manor where they were planning to kill her and me. Where I had found out Phillip was an alchemist and had been playing me.

It wasn't even a year ago, but it felt more like a decade had passed since then. And yet, the agony that rose in my chest with that memory as we climbed out of the SUV told me it seemed like yesterday.

"This way," Allen said, gesturing to the front door.

"Are you sure we can trust them?" Artan asked in a low voice. "What if we get in there and they lock us up inside?"

"They drank a potion to prove they are on our side," Ramon said. "Have a little faith." He patted Artan's chest before walking forward, toward the mansion.

Kane squeezed my hand. "Let's go."

A little wary, I let him lead the way into the house. Damara, who had been incredibly quiet, trailed behind us, the fire rope around her wrists tugging her forward with my magic.

The foyer with its round table and flower vase and curving staircase and beautiful glass chandelier screamed this was a normal house. I glanced to the sides—the living room and dining room all looked normal. But then Allen opened an invisible panel underneath the staircase, revealing stairs leading down.

Without a word, he went down first, followed by two other alchemists. The rest of them stayed upstairs, while we took a gamble and went down the narrow staircase.

The stairs ended in a wide corridor lined with closed doors—I couldn't even begin to imagine what was behind each one—and led to an archway and a room beyond.

Allen took us to that room. Wide and tall, the room

looked like a library, with shelves lining the walls and occupying the space. There weren't just books here. There were boxes, vials, herbs, bowls full of things that looked like clipped nails and bat wings and eyeballs—I pressed a hand over my queasy stomach.

From one of those shelves, Allen picked up a small red chest and brought it to us. "This is the Stone of the Tziganes," he said, opening the lid.

Damara stepped closer, and we gawked at the object on a black velvet cushion.

The Stone of the Tziganes was a crude heart-shaped red gemstone that had been separated into two halves. Each piece was attached to a thin golden chain with links in the shape of small leaves.

I could feel it. The thump of its power inside the stones, as if it was a real heartbeat.

"Incredible," I whispered.

"The chains were magically forged out of the petals of heart flowers," Allen said. "It can only be wielded by two heart maidens, not one."

Damara frowned. "Two heart maidens? That doesn't make sense. This is the first time in tzigane history that there are two heart maidens at the same time."

"Not really," Sheila said.

I stared at my grandmother. "What?"

"I don't know the details," she added quickly. "I've heard the legends that, many centuries ago, there were two heart maidens. I always thought it was just that, another legend."

Another legend based on the truth, as usual.

"According to our records, Anasztaz is one of the rulers of the underworld. He was brought to this world once, many centuries ago, by mistake. When he started wreaking havoc, a heart maiden wielded the Stone of the Tziganes to kill the titan," Allen explained. "But it was too much for her. The stone killed her."

I gasped. "What happened to Anasztaz?"

Allen went on, "Several enclaves got together and were able to contain the titan in a special but simple prison for a while, but it kept getting free and killing people."

"How did Anasztaz end up in his last prison?" I asked.

"It is said that the elder council of Shandor enclave, from where the previous heart maiden was from, tried a crazy idea," Allen said. "They divided the stone in two, hoping the next heart maiden could yield one half of it and destroy the titan once and for all. Meanwhile, they had to endure the titan's wrath whenever he escaped."

"They had to wait until a new heart maiden was born?" I asked, stunned.

"Not only born, but older too, capable of using her magic properly," Damara pointed out.

"Right," Allen agreed. "But after the stone was divided, it never worked again. The heart maiden wasn't able to make the stone work."

"What happened then?" my grandmother asked.

"Our records say that Saint Sara-la-Kali must have taken pity on your kind and sent another heart maiden to this world," the alchemist said. "Still, they had to wait until she was old enough to have control over her magic, but once she could do it, both heart maidens wore the half stones and were able to create a new prison and send it there."

"So, you're saying Damara and I need to wear these stones and work together to send Anasztaz back to its prison." I glanced at Damara. She was as rigid as a statue.

"Precisely," Allen said.

He extended the chest to us. Eyes fixed on the stones, Damara reached for it.

I slapped her hand away. "No."

She glared at me. "What the hell are you doing?"

I closed the lid to the chest. "You can't wear this. If it does what he's saying, then you'll be even more powerful and I won't be able to contain you."

"Dear Mirella, our powers are equal." She pulled her hands apart and the fire rope around her wrists broke off, becoming smoke that faded away. "You can't contain me. I've been playing nice because this is in my interest too."

I stared at her, a little upset, but not shocked. Deep down, I knew she could have broken free at any moment if she wanted to, but somehow, I hoped I was mistaken. Maybe because she was apart from Trina, and I had Kane by my side? I didn't know.

Although, she had stayed. She hadn't tried to escape, or tried to bargain with us. She was just going along, helping here and there with some useful information, and waiting.

Waiting for when she could save Trina.

I didn't like it. I really didn't.

"It'll only work if the two of you wear the necklaces," Allen said, his tone absolute, as if he was daring us not to. What? Then our deal would be broken?

I shook my head, more confused by the minute.

"Mirella," Damara started, her voice softer. "I know what you're feeling right now. Not in my two hundred and some years would I have dreamed of working side by side with you, but here I am, willing and ready." Her eyes filled with tears once more. "I need you and you need me. There's no other way."

By Saint Sara-la-Kali.

With a dark cloud swirling around my heart, I opened the chest again and reached for one of the stones. The power in it zapped into my fingertips, through my hand, and down my arm. Holy ... this shit was strong!

Even though it pained me and made every nerve in my body scream with agony, I handed the stone to her.

With a small smile, Damara took the necklace from me. She stared at the stone pendant for a moment, then slid the chain around her head.

"Your turn," Allen said.

My hand shook a little, but I held my anxiety back. I closed my hand around the stone and picked it up—power jolted into me. Watching Damara, I put on the necklace.

Another wave of power rolled through me and I felt it. I felt her. Before, when the fire heart fever was in control and I was easily connected to Damara, was nothing compared to now.

I could feel the fire magic swirling in her veins. I could hear her breathing, listen to her heartbeat.

I could hear her thoughts.

Get out of my head, she screamed.

I flinched, surprised with the intensity of her rage. I pulled back and rose thicker walls around my head. The last thing I needed was Damara rummaging through my thoughts too.

"What now?" Kane asked.

Allen's fists clenched. "Now, we open a portal to the underworld and kill Anasztaz."

21

As much as I would have loved going directly to the underworld to take Anasztaz out, I knew it was way too late and everyone was tired. So, we went back to camp.

With the red alchemists.

At first, the warriors who had been guarding the perimeter attacked us, but once they saw me, Kane, and the others, they lowered their weapons.

Though the expression in their faces told me they were utterly confused.

Me too, I wanted to tell them. Me too.

The rest of the tziganes didn't react well either. They gathered in the center of the camp, practically cowering, asking why they were here.

"Don't worry," I told them all, hoping they would let this one go. "They won't harm anyone. We have a spell in place, and they can't break it."

They didn't look relieved or understanding, but they didn't push it.

At first.

As the alchemists settled at the tree line, just outside the camp's north side, whispers reached my ears.

That I had already let Damara join us, now the alchemists. What was next? The revenants? Or even Anasztaz?

I tried ignoring it all, because people were scared—I was too—and they weren't in my shoes. The decisions I had to make ... they weren't easy. To be honest, I thought they would never be.

That was one of the reasons I sometimes hated being the heart maiden.

After stopping by the kitchen with Kane and greeting my mother and father, I went to Theron's tent. He was already sleeping, but Ellie was awake, seated beside his mattress, caring for him.

I knelt beside her. "How is he?"

"He's ... I don't know." She sighed. "We have to keep him sedated almost all the time, because he goes crazy when he realizes what happened. He doesn't want to accept it."

I had heard that Ryane had been able to stop him from dying after the revenant's bite, but the revenant's poison had spread, and he was now presenting several of the vampire's features—pale skin, sensitivity to the sun, elongated canines, and more.

By Saint Sara-la-Kali ... I now had a werewolf brother and a vampire one.

Next, I would turn into a mermaid and we would be quite the trio.

Despite wanting to joke about the subject to lighten the mood, it was impossible to. Theron would never be the same, and he might not accept his new self at first.

I placed my hand on her knee. "And how are you?"

Ellie was human, the only one among us, and she was here because she was my best friend, because I couldn't stay away from her and keep her from this life. And then there was Theron. She had fallen for Theron long ago. I couldn't imagine how hard it was to watch the man she loved becoming a vampire.

"I'm okay, I think." Her brows curled down. "I'm not afraid of him, but afraid for him. Remember how Ramon was shunned at first for being a werewolf? It'll be worse this time, because all revenants are evil and they killed many of your people."

"We'll help him," I said, and I meant it. "I'm here for you two, no matter what. Just let me know what I can do and I'll do it."

She turned a soft smile to me, a sad smile that didn't reach her eyes. "For now, just kick Anasztaz ass and bring back our friends."

I nodded. "I'll try."

I stayed with Ellie and Theron a few more minutes, but it was getting late. If we planned to go to the underworld first thing in the morning, I had to rest.

I groaned. I hated resting and sleeping lately. It was a waste of time, and I usually had nightmares and ended up not sleeping anyway.

Lost in my thoughts, I didn't notice when Damara stepped in my way.

"I was looking for you," she said.

It was so agonizing to see her walking among our people, no chains or ropes, and wearing a powerful stone around her neck. But I had decided to trust her, and I would try as hard as I could to honor that.

By Saint Sara-la-Kali, I really hoped she wouldn't betray us.

"What is it?" I asked, bracing myself.

Damara narrowed her eyes at me. "You're not wearing the necklace."

I patted my neckline, but I knew I wouldn't find anything there. "I took it off when we were leaving the alchemists' hideout." I patted one of the pockets in my uniform. "It's right here." She nodded, but didn't say anything. "So ... you wanted to talk to me."

"Right." She glanced up. From here, we couldn't see the moon, but there were many stars out, blanketing the night sky. "I wanted to apologize."

I ablinked, sure I hadn't heard her right. "What?"

Damara returned her gaze to me. "I wanted to say I'm sorry for all I've done to you and your people. I know nothing I say will ever fix it but I have to try. I was consumed with the magic and the madness and pure revenge, and I couldn't think straight. I couldn't handle what the council had put me through. It wasn't me. I had been gone for a long, long time. It was only after I found Trina and the madness started to retreat, slowly. And it was after she was taken from me that I realized what I had done." A tear rolled down her cheek. "I was an evil bitch, and I'll live the rest of my life paying for it." She wiped at her face furiously. "But I can't lose Trina, Mirella. I can't. If I do, I'll be a goner. The madness will consume me through my grief, and it'll be ten times worse than before. I don't want that. I don't want to be like that again."

She was right. I could never forgive everything she had done. But ... I didn't want to think of any buts. Not yet. If I ever gave Damara another chance, that would come later, after the fight with Anasztaz.

"Damara—"

"I was insane and hurting and gone for so long," she interrupted me, her voice breaking. "The only thing that made it all better was Trina. If we can't get her back ... then I don't want to live anymore."

Until yesterday, she was my number one enemy, and now I was feeling sympathy toward her. I hated this, because I wanted to remain wary of her. Cautious.

Originally, Damara wasn't a bad person. She became evil because of all the things that happened to her—having Emilian killed, being tortured by the council, being alone and mad, consuming too much heart flower by herself ... anyone would lose their minds like that.

I shook my head, not ready for this line of thought yet. "We'll get Trina back, Damara, I promise."

"One thing I learned from fighting you all of this time is that you're loyal to your friends. If you say we're going to rescue Trina, even if it's because of your friends, I believe you."

She was giving me way too much credit, which made me feel uncomfortable. "Go rest, Damara. We have a big fight tomorrow."

With a sigh, she nodded and walked away, toward her tent.

And I went looking for Kane.

All this talk about Trina and how Damara owed everything to her made me think and miss my own heart keeper way too much.

I found him where I left him—in the kitchen. But this time he wasn't eating, he was helping clean up.

"There you are," he said when he saw me. A warm smile adorned his full lips. "Everything okay?"

"I think so." I leaned against him. "Are you done here? 'Cause I want to curl up against you and sleep."

He planted a kiss on the top of my head. "Almost."

I helped, and fifteen minutes later, we walked to our tent, our hands linked. The original plan had been to snuggle and sleep, but once inside, we couldn't stop ourselves.

As if we were starving for each other, Kane and I made slow, sweet love.

Only after we were exhausted and sweaty and full of love did we curl up into each other and finally sleep.

22

____

AT SUNRISE, WE MARCHED TOWARD OUR LAST BATTLEFIELD. IT was ironic, because I had thought that yesterday too. What if this wasn't the last battle? The last fight? I didn't want to think about that.

It was a quiet morning, as if even the birds and insects knew our mood was tense. Jumpy.

We stopped by the edge of the crater. I dared lean over it and look down. Several yards down, the earth looked like sand in an hourglass, as if the slightest movement, would cause it to start crumbling into itself again.

"Are you two ready?" Kane asked, standing beside Damara and me.

The others formed a semicircle around us—Ramon, Artan, Dolan, Rye, Jayme, and many other warriors and some wolves. Allen was also here with his alchemists.

"Ready," Damara said, her tone firm, eager.

I hesitated. I couldn't explain why. Because of the danger ahead? Because we all could die? Because I had to trust

Damara and work with her? Pushing those thoughts away, I nodded. "I'm ready."

Damara and I held on to the stones and channeled our magic into them. The red stone warmed against my skin and a soft light shone from it.

Rye pointed at us. "Look!"

A thin black wall formed between Damara and me. It seemed made of dark light, or shimmering smoke.

"It's the portal," I whispered, reaching with my hand toward it. Allen had told us we would have the power to open a portal and reach Anasztaz, but it had sounded too crazy. It still was, even though I was looking right at it.

Before I could dip my fingers into the portal, Damara walked through it.

"Someone is in a rush," Artan muttered.

"Well, me too." Rye was the next one to step through the portal.

Then we all walked in.

The portal led to a ledge overlooking an abyss. Below, a river of lava billowed, with bubbles popping up, drops of lava reaching high. The heat brushed against my skin, but it didn't bother me. It did bother the others though. As we walked through the narrow path alongside the abyss, Rye wiped his sweaty forehead with his arm. Jayme took off his vest. Others sipped water.

I glanced back at my father, to check on him. I had asked him not to come, but he said he was an adult, older than me, and responsible for his actions. He wanted to come to help in any way, and nothing I said or did could stop him. Other than locking him up somewhere—the thought had crossed my mind.

We went down the path, until it cut through the earth, in

a narrow, dark tunnel, and emerged onto a wide ledge. Below was what resembled Greek ruins, with round pillars broken in half, crumbled domes over fallen archways, stone paths, and at the end of the room, a throne made of stone ~~and~~ with missing pieces.

And on it sat Anasztaz.

Right behind him, our friends and the other alchemists were seated on the rough pavement, tied with chains to each other and to tall columns flanking them.

My heart sank when I realized they weren't just seating, but they were leaning against each other, their heads lolled forward, as if they had no strength left.

Cora and Trina were among them.

Damara stepped forward, as if she would jump from the ledge and—I didn't even know what she had in mind. I caught her wrist and held her back. She glared at me and jerked free from my grasp.

As if sensing our presence, several fiends appeared among the ruins. The titan looked up at us.

Suppressing the sudden fear crawling up my spine, I led our group down through the broken stone stairs from the ledge, to an archway on the bottom.

I expected the fiends to attack before we walked halfway to the titan, but the fiends just hovered close to us. Waiting, teasing, instilling more fear in us.

Damara and I halted about ten feet from the bottom step leading up to Anasztaz's throne, and with our army behind us, we faced him.

"Anasztaz," Damara started, her voice loud and harsh. "Free our people, or suffer the consequences."

The titan let out a laugh that rumbled his entire body.

"Consequences? What will you do?" he asked in his rough, deep voice.

Flames appeared in her hands. "I'll destroy you."

Laughing some more, Anasztaz unfolded from the throne. "It's funny how you think you can take me down."

"We can," she assured him.

Anasztaz didn't seem amused by her statement.

Instead, he let out a roar that shook the walls.

Then, he attacked.

23

WE DIDN'T HAVE TIME TO THINK, BARELY TO REACT. ANASZTAZ jumped at us, while the fiends came from all sides. It quickly turned into a messy fight. The warriors and alchemists tackled the fiends; Kane, Ramon, Rye, and Artan ran to free the prisoners; Damara and I caught Anasztaz's attention.

I channeled my power, and the power of the Stone of the Tziganes, and attacked the titan, sending my fire directly at its chest, willing my magic to penetrate between the cracks of the rocks forming its body. Damara did the same, but with different spells.

Hoping she would follow my lead, I sent a fiery snake to him. It twisted up his body, tying him up. I opened my mind to Damara and told her to do the same, to reinforce my magic, so it would be strong and Anasztaz couldn't break it.

But she had her mind closed. Moreover, she sent thick stakes of fire toward him. The stakes found the cracks in his body, but they simmered out before doing any real damage.

This clearly wasn't working.

"I'm hungry," Anasztaz billowed, taunting us. He swept

his big hands at me, and I had to roll out of the way, so he wouldn't snatch me. I hit my back against a broken stone pillar and watched as the titan turned to Damara.

Around me, the fight wasn't going well. I could see a few bodies on the ground already, both tziganes and alchemists.

In the distance, I saw as Kane, Rye, Ramon, and Artan broke the chains holding the prisoners, but most of them didn't have any strength left to move. Taking advantage of that, fiends came at them. Ramon shifted into a wolf and lunged at one of the fiends, biting it on the chest. The fiend's body slackened to the ground, where it became smoke and disappeared.

Kane and Artan helped Ramon push the fiends back, while Rye watched over Cora, who like the others, was too pale and weak.

"Do something!" Damara yelled. I snapped my attention back to her and Anasztaz. The titan made another swipe at her. Damara brought up a wall of fire to stop it. But it didn't. The monster reached its arm through the wall and Damara had to scurry to the side to avoid being taken.

Once more, I channeled the power in the stone and threw a powerful jet of fire at the titan. He roared, but I didn't think the fire hurt him that much. That or he had a high pain threshold.

"Nothing seems to hurt it," I yelled back at Damara.

She slid past Anasztaz and came to my side. "Isn't this shit working?" she asked, holding the stone pendant.

"I can feel the power of the stone making my magic stronger, but it's not working," I said. "We can barely harm the titan."

With a growl, Anasztaz spun and came at us again. "There you are."

Because of his size, the titan was a little slower than we were, so it wasn't too hard to get out of his way. But running around like that was burning our energy and stamina. Soon, we would be too tired to keep going.

We needed a better plan.

Damara ran to the side and threw some fire bolts at the titan, grabbing his attention.

Out of nowhere, Artan appeared by my side. He took my hand in his. "Mirella ... I'm so, so sorry for everything I've done, for being such a jerk, and not supporting you more."

"Artan, what—"

"Just know that I love you. I'll always love you." He brought my hand to his lips and kissed my knuckles. "Now, kick his ass."

He took off.

Swerving around the titan, Artan threw a big jet of wind at the creature.

Letting out a roar, Anasztaz turned toward him. "What do we have here?"

"Come and get me, you big ugly monster." Artan sent another gust of wind at the titan, so strong, the titan swayed to the side. When the titan moved toward him, Artan moved too. He jumped over broken columns and cracked stone, and positioned himself away from everyone. He was cornered along the wall with Anasztaz right in front of him. In the distance, his eyes found mine. "Show me what you got!"

Damara stood by my side. "Now!"

She raised her hands and sent a powerful strike of fire at the titan.

For a moment, I couldn't move. I couldn't think. My mind was still trying to catch up with what Artan was doing.

He was sacrificing himself to give us an advantage.

My core shook.

"Mirella!" Damara screamed at me.

Mind foggy, I lifted my arms and—

Anasztaz swung his big, rocky hand and caught Artan, trapping the warrior in its hand.

He popped Artan in his mouth and ate him.

Artan was gone.

24

———

NO FIRE CAME OUT OF MY HANDS.

Instead, I fell on my knees, not believing what I had witnessed.

Artan. My first love, my first protector, the man who broke my heart, the stubborn and rage-inducing warrior, the drunk who drove everyone crazy ... in the end, he had done a noble thing.

A painful thing.

My chest cracked open.

Damara grabbed my arm and tugged me up. "Get yourself together and do something. He died to buy you time, so you could kill the damn titan. Then do it." She pointed to Anasztaz. The titan turned toward Kane, Ramon, Rye, Cora, Trina, and the other prisoners.

Kane.

Oh no.

The numbness and pain were gone, replaced by rage. This damn titan was going down.

An idea struck me like hot iron.

Eyes wide, I faced Damara. "The necklaces. The pendants once formed one single stone. We need to do it again."

Damara shook her head. "But you heard them. When it was only one stone, the heart maiden died."

I took off my necklace. "But there are two now. We'll use the stone together."

She stared at me as if I was crazy. Then, she pulled her necklace around her head. "What do we have to lose?"

I linked her hand in mine and brought my half of the stone close to hers. "Ready?"

She nodded. "Ready."

We joined the two pieces of the stone.

Power like I could never have imagined flowed into my veins and increased my magic tenfold, a million-fold.

Through our bond, Damara and I didn't have to talk. We barely had to think. We both lifted the stone in front of us, keeping it together, and sent a blast of fire at Anasztaz.

Like a tsunami, the fire devoured it in mere seconds. The titan roared and stomped around, trying to get rid of the fire engulfing its body. The ground shook with the titan, the precarious columns and archways groaning as they moved too, threatening to fall.

"More," I said, my voice detached.

More fire came out of the stone and enveloped the titan, until finally, it stopped moving. Like a big, heavy tree trunk, the titan fell to the ground, and dust and dirt blew away.

Damara and I lowered the stone and the fire turned into embers. The titan's rocky body was dark orange from the fire. But a moment later, the rocks crumbled into small rubble.

The titan was gone.

Its fiends disappeared.

We had won.

Despite all our loses, we won.

SOMEHOW, WE MADE IT OUT OF THE UNDERWORLD. SOMEHOW, we brought our friends back. Somehow, we carried the bodies of the dead. Somehow, we made it back to the camp.

I didn't remember most of it.

What I really remembered well after the battle and coming back was the funeral. We found a nice area beside the stream near the camp and buried the dead.

Artan included.

During the funeral we had after, Artan was honored as a hero. He had sacrificed his life so we could save so many. It broke my heart that it had to be this way.

Ryane was inconsolable. She clung to Tomas and sobbed nonstop. Poor girl had lost her father, her grandmother, and now her brother. If she started hating me, I wouldn't blame her. After all, the mess began after I showed up in their lives.

But I tried remembering it was done now. All the bad stuff was behind us.

The only things left were to deal with Allen and his alchemists, and Damara, and then go back to Lovell.

After the funeral, all I wanted was to find a bed and go to sleep and pretend nothing ever happened. When I woke up, the world would be great again. Perfect.

But life wasn't perfect. It would never be.

Ramon, Kane, and I met Allen in the main tent.

"I can honestly say the happenings of the last couple of days changed us all," Allen said. "From now on, I promise my alchemists won't harm any tziganes ever again."

I nodded. His alchemists. Unfortunately, he couldn't

speak for hundreds, thousands of others, just waiting to snatch and kill us. "I'm glad."

He grimaced. "But to work on our potions, we still need tzigane blood ..."

"I know, and in exchange, we will give you a small supply each month, if you promise to not just keep the peace, but to use these potions for good."

"Sounds fair," Allen said.

After we were done with the alchemists, Damara and Trina entered the tent. Holding hands, they stood across the table from us.

"I'm sorry," Damara whispered. Besides last night when she apologized to me, I had never seen her looking so sheepish. This look didn't suit her. "I know I can never be forgiven for all the crimes I committed and the pain I caused."

"I know you probably intend to punish us for all that happened," Trina started. "But—"

"Your punishment is to leave this area," I said, cutting her off. "You two are to live simply and quietly. I don't want to hear any news about you two. Not bad news, at least."

Damara and Trina exchanged a glance, then nodded at me.

"We accept that punishment," Damara said. "Also, I wanted to let you know, I won't take any more heart flowers. Even if one sprouts right at my feet, I won't touch it."

I frowned, glad about that decision, but curious. "Why?"

"Because the magic in the flowers was what extended my life," she said. "I don't want that anymore. I want to live a long life, but with Trina. When she dies, I want to die too."

Trina smiled at her.

My heart squeezed for them. I honestly hoped they could create a better, happier life for themselves.

Trina looked at us. "If you allow it, we'll leave now."

For some reason, I felt sad. "You may go. Please, be good, and be happy."

They nodded at me, then walked out of the tent.

"Who is next?" Ramon asked, as if we had an agenda and our next appointment would show up at any minute.

"I think we're done," Kane said. "All we need to do now is move back to Lovell."

I wondered what the state of my cabin was. I hadn't been there in ... I didn't even know how long. A couple of days? A couple of years? I was so tired of fighting, it seemed I had been doing it for a century.

"What about you?" I asked Ramon.

"Now that Damara is out of the game, and the closest alchemists became our allies, I don't think there are many dangers out there," Ramon said. "We'll go back to our den, even though it's still a mess."

"Lovell is probably like that too," Kane said.

"Right." Ramon nodded. "But no matter what, it's home, you know?"

Home.

There were moments during these past nine months when I thought I had finally found my home, but it had been all lies. All brief reprieves, to tease me, to break me.

But this time, this time it might be true.

This time, there were no more eminent enemies, no evil, no upcoming fights.

This time, I may be able to finally relax.

I let out a long breath. "Let's go home."

25

———

LIFE COULDN'T BE THIS PERFECT. IT HAD TO BE A DREAM. BUT no matter how many times I pinched myself, nothing changed.

Four months ago, we moved back to Lovell. As we expected, the place was a mess, and because of our severely reduced numbers, it took us a while to fix everything.

But things got better from there.

Because there were many houses empty now, the Bellville people spread out, except for Sheila and Neil. Marie and Anne moved to a small house across the street, while Jayme, Brina, and their baby had taken a big house a few streets over —rumor was that Jayme wanted a lot more kids.

Theron finally accepted he was some sort of vampire now. He could be out in daylight, but he didn't like it, saying it made him feel uncomfortable. Ellie had officially moved in to the enclave—more specifically, to Theron's new house.

Ryane was living at her big family's house with Tomas. They had gotten married about two months ago, but since she had just lost her family members and wasn't feeling up to it, we didn't hold a big ceremony for them. She was now the head of the infirmary, and she was training Ellie to help her.

Cora finally surrendered to Rye. I guess that after that horrible experience, she realized she could have died and she didn't want to hold him at arm's length anymore. They too had moved in together, and there were talks of an upcoming wedding.

Ramon and his wolves moved back to their den. They seemed happy there, though I wished it was a little closer so we could visit each other more often. Especially now that Violet had a beautiful baby boy, and I wanted to squeeze my nephew all the time.

Although I liked my cabin at the edge of the enclave, I too took a medium-sized house closer to the main square, and Kane had moved in with me, obviously. I loved waking up beside him every morning.

In the past four months, I had sent the monthly supply of blood to the alchemists, and they had kept their word so far. From the reports I received, they were not only behaving, but keeping other alchemists from coming too close. It was like they had claimed this area, and while we maintained peace, I was okay with that.

As for Damara and Trina, they also had kept their word. I hadn't heard from them. I had sensed one heart flower since they left, and I half-expected to find Damara coming for it too, for not resisting the call and the alluring magic, but she hadn't come. I had found the flower and brought it back without any problems.

Because of our loses, I had changed the council members slightly—Ryane had taken Artan's place and joined Kane, my mother, my father, my grandmother, Theron, Ellie, Cora, and Rye. I had daily meetings with them, to check on everything.

So far, they were doing a great job and the tziganes seemed happy.

With all the past invasions, we had also increased security around the enclave. We now had a tall wall around the entire area. This wall was enchanted with strong magic, ~~and~~ cameras and alarm triggers. The elder tziganes didn't like the use of technology, but what other option did we have? Magic wasn't infallible, as we had learned, neither was technology, but maybe together, they would work all right.

So far, everything was perfect—just like this day.

I knocked on the door of my mother's bedroom and pushed it open. "Are you ready?"

My mother stood in front of the tall standing mirror. She looked beautiful in a cream-colored gown and yellow embroidery. Her long hair was up in an intricate bun, with yellow flowers woven between the strands. Her makeup was light and emphasized the traces of her beautiful face.

"I think so," she said, turning to me. Her hands shook slightly.

"Don't tell me you're nervous," I teased her.

"Well, I might be old for this, but it's my first time."

I smiled at her.

I should have known there was more going on between my mother and my father than spending time together and caring for their children. It turned out, they had been together for a few months now, but they didn't want to bother us with that, at least not until we all could breathe properly again.

Once we defeated Anasztaz, sent Damara away, and moved back to Lovell, they announced their relationship, and that they would like to get married.

My father had been married to Theron and Ramon's

mother before, but my mother had never gotten married. I honestly believed after all the years she lived raising me, hiding me, there was only one man in her heart.

And now she was marrying him.

"Then let's not be late, or you'll miss it." I took her shaking hand in mine and guided her out.

The streets were empty, even though it was a beautiful and unusually warm fall evening. That was because everyone was in the main square, waiting for the bride.

At the edge of the square, I met Theron and Ramon, both looking fancy in black slacks, white shirts, and yellow sashes.

"We got it from here," Theron said, taking my mother's arm.

I smiled at the trio. "See you in a bit."

Then, I walked to another entrance to the square, where my father stood with Sheila.

"There you are," my father said. He looked as nervous as my mother. "Everything okay?"

"Everything is perfect." I linked my arm to his, then looked at my grandmother. "We're ready."

"Great." She walked into the square, by the corridor formed by the chairs set up in the square, and stopped at the improvised platform in front of the fountain.

She nodded at the musicians positioned to the side of the platform, and they began playing. A melodious slow flamenco song echoed through the square.

"That's our cue," I said, tugging my father forward.

Under the watchful gazes of our friends, my father and I walked down the aisle and stopped at the platform beside my grandmother. Next, Ramon and Theron escorted my mother in.

My mother and my father locked gazes and didn't break

them, even as my brothers handed my mother to our father, as Sheila presided over the ceremony, through their vows, until finally, they had to greet the guests.

My heart warmed at their happiness and love.

Seated in the first row beside me, Kane leaned closer and placed a kiss on my cheek.

I frowned at him. "What was that for?"

"Can't I kiss my soulmate?"

A smile spread over my lips. "Always."

He pressed his lips to mine for a brief moment, then took my hand in his. "The party is starting." He glanced around, and I followed suit. The tziganes were moving to the other side of the square, where there were tables with plenty of food and drinks, and a space for dancing.

We watched as my father and mother shared a dance. On the next song, more people joined them.

"They seem so happy," I muttered, feeling happy myself. "They all do."

"True." Kane slid his hand in mine. "I would like to dance with my heart maiden."

"Hm, you're lucky, because your heart maiden would really like to dance with her heart keeper." Kane brought my hand to his lips and pressed a soft kiss on the inside of my wrist, before standing up and pulling me with him.

In no time, we were on the dance floor, in each other's arms, swaying with the beat of the song, and surrounded by our family and friends.

If this wasn't paradise, I didn't know what was.

I stood on my tiptoes and brushed my lips to Kane's. "I love you."

One corner of his lips tugged up. "I love you more."

Heart full, I rested my head on his shoulder and let him spin us around, weaving through the crowd.

We all had gone through so much, lost so much, changed so much, but we emerged stronger, and I knew that if any other danger came at us, we would face it together, without fear, sure that we would succeed.

But I hoped no danger found us, because right now, right at this moment, life was perfect and I wished it would stay like that forever.

THANK YOU

THANK YOU FOR READING *WAR MAIDEN*!

Reviews are very important for authors. If you liked my book, please consider leaving a review on your preferred online store and/or on goodreads, please!

DID YOU LIKE THIS BOOK? YOU CAN CHECK OUT OTHER BOOKS of mine:

The Demon Kiss (Rite World: Blackthorn Hunters Academy Book 1): a fast-paced story about a young woman who finds out she's a demon hunter, and the half-demon intent on protecting her against all evil.

The Vampire Heir (Rite World 1: Rite of the Vampire): a dark and mysterious paranormal romance about a vampire and a young woman with a secret.

The Warlock Lord (Rite World 4: Rite of the Warlock): a thrilling and kick-ass paranormal romance about a werewolf and warlock.

Destiny Gift (The Everlast Series book 1): a post-apocalyptic urban fantasy series about a young woman with a special power that can save the world.

Don't forget to sign up for my Newsletter to find out about new releases, cover reveals, giveaways, and more!

If you want to see exclusive teasers, help me decide on covers, read excerpts, talk about books, etc, join my reader group on Facebook: Juliana's Club!

ABOUT THE AUTHOR

While USA Today Bestselling Author Juliana Haygert dreams of being Wonder Woman, Buffy, or a blood elf shadow priest, she settles for the less exciting—but equally gratifying—life as a wife, a mother, and an author. She resides in North Carolina and spends her days writing about kick-ass heroines and the heroes who drive them crazy.

Subscribe to her mailing list to receive emails of announcement, events, and other fun stuff related to her writing and her books: www.bit.ly/JuHNL

For more information:
www.julianahaygert.com

facebook.com/julianahaygert
twitter.com/juliana_haygert
instagram.com/juliana.haygert

ALSO BY JULIANA HAYGERT

www.julianahaygert.com/books/

Free
Into the Darkest Fire
Tested

Rite World: Blackthorn Hunters Academy
The Demon Kiss (Book 1)
The Hunter Secret (Book 2)
The Soul Bond (Book 3)
The Shadow Trials (Book 4)
The Infernal Curse (Book 5)

Rite World
The Vampire Heir (Book 1)
The Witch Queen (Book 2)
The Immortal Vow (Book 3)
The Warlock Lord (Book 4)
The Wolf Consort (Book 5)
The Crystal Rose (Book 6)

The Fire Heart Chronicles
Heart Seeker (Book 1)

Flame Caster (Book 2)

Sorrow Bringer (Book 3)

Earth Shaker (Novella)

Soul Wanderer (Book 4)

Fate Summoner (Book 5)

War Maiden (Book 6)

The Everlast Series

Destiny Gift (Book 1)

Soul Oath (Book 2)

Cup of Life (Book 3)

Everlasting Circle (Book 4)

Willow Harbor Series

Hunter's Revenge (Book 3)

Siren's Song (Book 5)